Friend or Foe

DEBBIE ANDERSON

Copyright © 2018 by Debbie Anderson
All rights reserved.
ISBN-10:1979475849
ISBN-13: 978-1979475846

DEDICATION

I dedicate this book to Maureen Brown, my mentor, teacher, and friend. She believed I could be a writer before I did, suggesting I take this subject and turn it into a novel. Unfortunately, she passed before I could get it published. I miss you, Maureen. This one's for you!

ACKNOWLEDGMENTS

Thank you to my wonderful family. First, to my children, Josh, Janie, and Nathan. Who have always inspired me and who are gracious enough to allow me to use their exploits, although exaggerated, in my books.

To my brothers, sisters, brother-in-law, sisters-in-law, nieces and nephews, whose support and encouragement keep me going.

To my parents, who love me and stand beside me in all my adventures, this not being the least of those.

And finally, to my fellow writers at my Writing for Fun writer's club, who listened to every word of this book as it progressed, providing support, encouragement, editing, and constructive criticism for my work in progress. Thank you for your help.

1

Janie forced one eye open and looked at the alarm clock. Her focus fighting to come to the surface of her still-sleeping brain.

Ten fifty-seven.

Her eyelid, unable to stay open on its own, fell back to its previous position – closed. Suddenly, both eyes were wide open and staring at the clock.

Ten fifty-eight.

"Ten fifty-eight!" Janie jumped from her comfy bed. "How can it be ten fifty-eight?" She checked the alarm clock. She had forgotten to set it when she crawled into bed a few hours ago after studying most of the night.

Standing in the middle of the room, she looked in one direction and then the other trying to decide what to do first.

"Good thing I got my clothes ready last night. I'll take a quick shower, grab a bagel, and I'm outta here. Wait. I did put the clothes in the dryer, didn't I?" Running to the dryer she went through her movements from the night before. Study. Fix dinner while studying. Wash clothes while studying. Study some more. Study. Study. Study. By the time she reached the dryer, she was in a full-blown panic. She jerked open the door and …

"Noooo!"

Janie pulled the clothes from the washing machine and

threw them into the dryer. She reached for a dryer sheet. Empty! She started the dryer and ran to the bathroom.

Turning the shower on full blast, she

stepped in, then jumped out as the ice-cold spray hit her. Shivering she took a deep breath, adjusted the temperature, and climbed back in.

"Okay, I'm running late. I can still make this work. The first exam is at twelve-thirty. I can make it if I leave by noon. Dry my hair, do makeup, grab a bagel, and out the door. I can do this."

Janie stepped out of the shower and reached for the towel—which wasn't there.

She ran to the linen closet and pulled out a towel, drying herself as she made her way back to the bathroom. Next, she half-dried her hair–mostly damp with a few dry strands on top. Applied makeup, covering up a huge pimple that obviously came up overnight. *I'll do a quick touch-up at school.*

"Next, grab the clothes from the dryer." They were slightly wrinkled and very staticy. *Is anything going to go right today?*

In the kitchen, she grabbed the coffeepot

and reached for the can of Folgers. Empty. She pulled on her shoes and grabbed the bagel bag. It was empty, too.

She looked at the clock. Eleven fifty-three. "If I leave right now, I can grab a coffee on my way to class."

Out the door, into the car, and away she went. Her first exam was an oral presentation. She hated oral exams, but she needed to pass this course for her degree. Janie rehearsed her presentation as she drove.

Stopping at a light, she noticed half a bagel in the passenger seat from the day before. For a second, she considered eating it. She was hungry, but when she picked it up, it was rock hard.

The light changed, and she resumed her route. Rolling down the window, she tossed out the hockey-puck-like bagel and continued practicing her presentation.

Suddenly, flashing lights appeared in her

rear-view mirror. Janie looked at the speedometer–she wasn't speeding. *He must be going after someone else.* She sighed, relieved. She pulled her car to the curb so the officer could go around her.

The police officer parked his motorcycle behind her.

Grabbing her purse, she pulled out her license, rolled down the window, and waited for the officer.

"Ma'am, can I see your license and proof of insurance?"

Janie handed him her identification.

"Ms. Alexander, did you throw something out of your car?"

"Yes sir, it was an old, hard bagel, but it's not littering. The birds will eat it." She beamed her brightest smile, showing all her teeth.

"Ma'am, I was behind you. The bagel hit me in the face. Please don't do that again. It hurt!"

Janie felt her cheeks flushing. *Of course, it did!*

"I'm sorry, officer. I won't do it again. Are you okay?" What was the correct thing to do when you accosted a police officer with a bagel?

The officer nodded. He handed back her license and insurance documents.

"Have an enjoyable day, Ma'am. Keep the baked goods in the car." He gave her a smile; a quick salute and was gone.

"I can't believe this." A glance at her watch informed her it was twelve o'eight. No time to stop for coffee now. She put her car in gear and steered away from the curb.

Janie pulled into a parking place at twelve twenty-three.

No time to stop in the ladies' room for a quick once-over. She ran to class and through the open door. Twelve twenty-nine.

She took her seat as the teacher shut the door.

2

Janie left the class feeling good about her oral exam. She knew her subject, projected well and some of the other students smiled during the presentation. In fact, many students were snickering and looking at each other. They were laughing at the presentation, right?

Her next exam was in two hours. She decided to go to Starbucks and wait there for her next class. She would get a cup of coffee and try to relax.

Janie ran across the parking lot to her car. She really needed to get away from here for a while. She pulled out of her parking space, nearly hitting another car. She quickly waved; responding to the one-finger salute the other driver gave her and took off.

A few minutes later, she was ordering a *Grande Carmel Macchiato* with an extra shot, whipped cream and a dash of cinnamon and a banana-nut muffin the size of her head. She found a table and dumped her books while she waited for her order.

The coffee smelled wonderful. Breathing in the rich aroma, she began to relax and forget about this morning. Once she had her caffeine fix, she would be just fine. Closing her eyes, she took a long sip of the amber brew.

She nibbled a bit of her muffin and tried to relax. She blew on her coffee and took another "Just what I needed," she purred. Taking another sip, she closed her eyes and enjoyed the warmth as it slowly wound its way down her throat. "Mmmmm." A sly smile slid onto her face. Anything this good had to be sinful.

"Looks like you're really enjoying your coffee. What did you order? I might want what you're having."

Janie's eyes popped open, and she found a man in uniform standing in front of her.

"You," she exclaimed, recognizing the uniform, and the man in it, as the police officer from earlier, the one she hit with the bagel.

The officer offered her a crooked smile. "I didn't mean to bother you."

"No, you're not bothering me. You just surprised me," she said, blushing.

"I'm Shawn," the officer stated, extending his hand.

Janie shook his hand and smiled. "Small world."

"Do you have a name?"

"Oh, sorry. I'm Janie. It's been a strange day." The officer was quite handsome. That dimple in his cheek was charming. "Would like to join me?"

Shawn pulled up a stool and set his coffee

on the table.

"You're not following me, are you?" Janie asked as she flashed him a brilliant smile.

"No. But as I pulled up, I noticed your car."

"Did anyone lose their panties?" The question came from the front of the store, by the counter. Puzzled, Janie and Shawn looked at each other, then turned toward the voice in unison. The UPS man was standing there holding up a pair of red, lacy panties. The barista was laughing.

"I found them lying here in front of the counter," he explained.

"They're not mine!" The barrister waved his hands and stepped back from the counter as he laughed.

"Anyone lose their panties?" the UPS man asked a little louder, holding them up for the rest of the restaurant to see. The customers were laughing and looking around at the discovery, curious to see if anyone would claim the prize.

Suddenly, Janie started choking. The red lace panties with the little bow in the front. Her favorite pair. What were they doing here? Oh. My. Gosh. They must have stuck to my jeans when I pulled them from the dryer.

Shawn patted her on the back. "Are you okay?"

She looked at Shawn and nodded, trying to catch her breath. "I'm fine. I just swallowed wrong."

She could feel the color move up her neck, past her chin, and to her forehead. She was sure the roots of her blonde hair were blushing. How embarrassing! As much as she loved those panties, she was not about to admit they were hers.

"That's got to be a great story," Shawn said, nodding toward the panties. Janie nodded and performed an imaginary eye roll in her head. Then she realized the panties were probably stuck to her pants while she gave her presentation. Her smile froze as she thought about it. Good thing the semester was over. She would have to change her appearance completely before she could ever face anyone from that class again.

She took another gulp of her coffee.

Shawn reached over, removed the foam from her upper lip with his finger, and licked it off. Janie melted a little. He really was good-looking.

"Well, I better get back to work," Shawn said. "It was really great to meet you." Looking down at her muffin, he added, "You are going to eat that, aren't you? You don't plan on hurling it at me later?"

Janie rolled her eyes for real. "I plan to eat it, thank you, but I may change my mind. You never know." She grinned at him with a glimmer of mischief in her eye.

"I think you may need someone to watch out for you," he said. "I'm free Sunday. It would be a real drag, but if you would agree to go out with me, I'll volunteer for the job," he teased.

"Well, I don't know," she stated soberly. "I'm not one to let just anyone watch out for me. What would people think? Me, going out with a cop."

"I know it could be an inconvenience, and I can only imagine the rumors." He rubbed his chin. "I guess I could wear civilian clothes, so no one would know I'm a police officer. But what would people say when they see me having dinner with a notorious bagel slinger?"

Janie gave him a punch in the arm. He rubbed the spot as if she had really hurt him. "I guess I might be willing to risk it if you are."

"Good. You better give me your number before we both change our minds." They both laughed. Janie couldn't help but stare at his dimple. *He's kinda sexy*, she thought as she wrote down her number.

"Around seven?"

"Hmm?" Janie asked, hypnotized by the dent in his cheek.

"Sunday? Around seven?" Shawn reminded her.

"Oh! Sorry, something distracted me for a minute."

Shawn frowned and looked around to find what was distracting her.

"Your dimple!" Janie blurted. "I was distracted by your dimple. It's really cute."

It was Shawn's turn to blush. He ran his hand through his thick, dark hair. "Thanks. So, at seven o'clock, on Sunday. I'll call you."

"I'll look forward to it." Janie watched him walk to the door. "He even looks good from behind," she said aloud. Shawn turned and gave her a small wave. She waved back, wondering if he heard her. "I have to stop talking to myself." She took another bite of her muffin. "What a great day." She picked up her book but did not study. Instead, she started planning what she would wear Sunday night.

3

Sadie's, a cute little bistro near campus, was a popular hangout for the college crowd. Janie had agreed to meet her friend Heather for an after-exam celebration. As she walked in, she saw her friend in a back booth, waving to her.

"'Bout time," Heather teased as Janie slid into the red vinyl booth.

Janie grinned. "So, have you ordered yet?"

"Of course not. I didn't want anyone to think I was eating alone."

"You wouldn't have been alone for long."

Janie nodded to a table with several good-looking males, all of which openly stared at them. "Some of them are really cute."

Heather wrinkled her nose. "Not interested. I've sworn off men."

"Until the next one asks you out," Janie teased.

Heather recently broken up with her boyfriend and was still nursing her broken heart. "Not interested," she insisted.

"How did your exams go?"

"Fine. My calculus exam was the worst, but I think I passed it. How about you? How did your presentation go? I know you were worried about it."

"I don't know," Janie said. "I think the presentation itself was fine. But you won't believe what happened." She explained how, unbeknownst to her, her panties stuck to her jeans when she took them out of the dryer. Causing them to cling to her jeans throughout the presentation and all the way to Starbucks.

"Then, the UPS guy came into Starbucks, picked them up from the floor, and asked if anyone had lost their panties!"

"Stop! Stop! I'm going to pee my pants!" cried Heather.

"It gets worse," Janie continued. "They were my favorite panties! No way was I going to claim them in front of everyone! And this nice guy had just sat down at my table when this was happening!"

Heather fought to catch her breath. "O-Oh really? So, who is this nice guy? Anyone I know?"

"I don't think so. He's a police officer. The same one I hit with a bagel earlier this morning."

"Wait. What? You hit a police officer with a bagel? Why?"

"I didn't mean to. I tossed a dried-up bagel, which was on the seat in my car, out the window, and it hit this cop. He pulled me over and said not to do it again."

Heather couldn't stop laughing. She was holding her side, bent over, with tears streaming down her face. She shook her head at Janie, sticking her hand out in a stop signal. "No more! I can't take any more!"

By this time, Janie was laughing, too. It really was funny when you thought about it. Taking a deep breath, Heather wiped the tears from her face. "We should order. Do you know what you want?"

"A bagel," replied Janie, and the laughing started again.

The girls ordered Sadie's Special Burgers, curly fries, and beer.

"Janie, I don't know anyone who can get themselves into so much trouble in one morning. Tell me more about this police officer. He was cute, huh?"

"Yeah, pretty cute. Tall, dark hair, blue eyes, nice butt."

"Nice butt?"

"Get your mind out of the gutter. I saw him walk away, that's all. He had a nice butt."

"So, are you going to see him again?"

"We have a date Sunday night. He's supposed to call me."

"Maybe he'll call while you're here with me?"

"Maybe. But let's not forget why we're here—the end of exams—and school. Where are those beers?"

As if on cue, the server sat two frosty mugs on the table. "Here, here!" replied Heather, and the two girls clinked their glasses together and had a sip.

"I hope our food gets here soon. I'm starving," said Janie. Before Heather could respond, the server appeared with their order.

The girls talked about school, their exams, Heather's ex-boyfriend, and the dreamy cop that was to call later, as they ate their huge, juicy, hamburgers and salty fries.

Dipping the last of the fries in catsup and popping it in her mouth, Janie leaned back in her seat. "That was good. I'll just roll on out to my car and head for home. At least I'm done with studying."

"I won't need to eat for the rest of the week." Heather patted her flat belly. "You better call and let me know what happens with your new suitor."

"You know I will."

"I want details!"

"Of course you do!"

With a quick hug, they said their goodbyes and headed for their cars.

4

Day transitioned into night. Janie drove her secondhand, red Corolla toward home. The moon glowed through the trees, lighting the street ahead of her. Janie relaxed and sang along to oldies on the radio.

She was belting out the chorus to Love Me Do with the Beatles when she realized her cell phone was playing her current ringtone, the theme from Jaws.

Da-Da, Da-Da, …

Glancing at her phone caller ID, she saw it was Heather. "I'll call her when I get home."

Da-Da, Da-Da …

Janie frowned at the offending electronic sitting on her passenger seat. Picking it up, she saw it was Heather–again.

"What the …?" Janie edged over to the curb. But before she could return the call …

Da-Da, Da-Da …

Janie grabbed the phone. "Heather? What's wrong? Are you okay?"

"Ah, sorry. Should I call back later?"

It was Shawn. Janie smiled and blushed. "No, I'm sorry. My friend keeps calling, and I just saw her. I'm sure it's nothing …" She realized she was giving him way too much information. He didn't care about all that. Taking a deep breath, she started again. "I'm sorry. What's up?"

"I was just following up with you. I really enjoyed meeting you today. I know you're in the car. Did you pull over?"

"I did. I'm safe on the side of the road."

"I won't keep you. Would you like to go out earlier on Sunday?"

"Sure, that'd be fine." Janie pictured the handsome officer with the cute dimple.

"Dress casual. I've got a fun day planned. Can I pick you up around eleven?"

"No. I'll meet you." She had a strict policy of never letting anyone pick her up for a first date. She wanted to get to know them first.

"Okay. How about the parking lot at Wal-Mart?"

"Perfect! Eleven o'clock it is!"

"Great! I look forward to seeing you again."

"Me too." Janie disconnected the call, wondering what he had planned.

Da-Da, Da-Da ...

Janie looked at the screen. It was Heather again.

"Heather? What's wrong?"

"I've been calling and calling you. Why didn't you answer?"

"Uh—I'm driving. Besides, I just saw you. What could be so important?"

"Okay. Are you stopped?" Heather sounded weird.

"Yes, I pulled over. What's wrong?"

"Are your doors locked?"

"No. But I'll lock them if it will make you feel better." Janie reached across the car to push down the lock button. "You're worrying me."

"I don't want to scare you or anything. It's just someone followed you from Sadie's."

"Yeah, right." Janie replied with a nervous laugh. "Wait, you are kidding, aren't you?"

"I'm perfectly serious. I saw this big black truck follow you out of the parking lot and down the street. I got a bad feeling about it, so I tried to follow, but it lost me." Heather spoke fast and sounded scared.

Janie looked around. "Heather, I don't see any black truck. I'm sure no one is following me."

"Please, be careful. I really got a bad vibe."

"I'll be careful. Did you see who was driving this truck?"

"No. It had tinted windows. I couldn't see inside."

"Okay. I'm sure it was nothing."

"I hope you're right. Be careful!"

"I will. I'll call you when I get home," Janie assured her.

Disconnecting the call, she pulled away from the curb. She had to admit she was a little spooked herself. That wasn't like Heather. Heather was very down to earth. She didn't scare easily.

Janie checked her rear-view mirror as she drove. The nearest vehicle was at least a block away and it looked like a car, not a truck. *I'm sure everything is fine.* She had planned on stopping at the grocery store on her way, but now she just wanted to get home. This entire day had been a little baffling. She glanced up at the full moon and groaned. It seemed to glow a little brighter as she watched. Janie frowned. "You're letting your imagination get away from you. It's just a full moon, don't make it into something it's not." As she watched, it seemed to brighten again.

Janie felt a little foolish, but mostly she was anxious. She continued home, checking her mirrors, watching for a black truck. She felt relieved when she finally pulled into her parking lot. She sat there for a minute, taking deep breaths and trying to calm down. Darn that Heather.

Pushing the creaky car door open, she stepped out into the warm night air. She winked up at the moon. "Everything is fine. What a fool I am! Scaring myself like that."

Just then, a large, black truck slowly rolled by. Janie's eyes widened as she saw the darkened windows. No one in her apartment complex had a black truck.

Picking up her purse and phone from the car seat, she ran toward her apartment. Suddenly, her foot caught on a crack in the sidewalk, and she found herself flying. She hit the ground hard, scraping her arms and knees. Frantically, she looked around her. The black truck had stopped just a few feet away.

Pulling herself to her feet, she performed an awkward limp-run to her door. Her hands shook so badly that she kept missing the lock with her keys. Risking a glance behind her, she saw the truck was still there. Just sitting there! The key found the slot and Janie opened the door, slamming and locking the deadbolt behind her. She leaned against the door, trying to catch her breath. *Who in the world was that?*

Janie peeked out the window that faced the parking lot. The truck hadn't budged. Quickly, she let go of the blinds. Stepping away from the window, she tried to calm herself so she could think rationally. Should she call the police?

"And tell them what? A black truck parked in my parking lot? I didn't even see it following me. Maybe a new tenant moved in and it's his truck. That's it. It's just another tenant." Janie crept back to the window; the truck was still there. "Of course, it's there, Goofball. Whoever it is, lives here now."

If he lives here, why didn't he get out of his truck?

"I'm sure there is a perfectly good explanation," Janie assured herself. *Sure, like he followed you here and is waiting for you to go to bed so he can break in and kill you!* Janie quickly moved away from the window. She checked the locks on the door. She checked the windows.

"A weapon. I need a weapon. What if he manages to get in? I'll need to defend myself." Frantically, she looked for something to use as a weapon. She pulled the umbrella from the closet. No, that wouldn't do any good. It folded at the first sign of a strong wind. Going to the kitchen, she grabbed a large, sharp knife from the knife block on the counter. Yes, that would work. Would she be able to use it? Her shoulders sagged as she thought about jabbing someone with a knife. Surely, she could use it if she were being attacked, wouldn't she? She sat the knife on the counter; she'd try to find something else.

Da-Da, Da-Da, ...

Janie grabbed her phone and breathlessly answered. "Hello?"

"Thank God! Are you okay? You didn't call me!"

Heather, I forgot to call Heather.

"I'm okay. I'm sorry. I was just trying to find a weapon."

"I knew it!" Heather yelled. Then whispering, she continued, "Are you alone? Is someone trying to break in? Are they already in? Should I call 9-1-1?"

"Don't call anyone. Why are you whispering? Yes, I'm alone. No one is trying to break in. I'm just a little anxious is all. You scared me with all your talk about a black truck following me."

"Sorry 'bout that. When I saw that truck following you, I got goosebumps. So, you didn't see anything?"

"I didn't see anyone following me but ..."

"I knew it! What happened?"

"Nothing. It's just ... well, a black truck with tinted windows did pull into my parking lot. I didn't see anyone get out."

"OMG! Janie, you need to get out of there. What if he breaks in? He could hurt you or worse! Oh Janie, please come over here and stay with me until we know what's going on. I don't like you being alone!"

"Heather, if whoever is in that black truck was following me and is still in the truck, don't you think I'd be safer in my locked apartment?" Heather was quiet as she thought about the situation.

"Really, I'll be fine. The doors are locked. I've got a knife."

"A knife?" shrieked Heather.

"It's better than my umbrella! It's the last

resort, but it's here if I need it."

"I don't like this. I don't like it at all."

"Don't worry, I'll be fine. I've got my phone. I'll call the police the first sign of anyone trying to break in. Then, I'll call you. Okay?"

"Okay. But I won't be able to sleep. I worry about you."

"I know you do. It will be fine. I think I'm going to make myself some chamomile tea and try to find a great old movie on TV. I think it's Cary Grant week on TCM."

"You and your old movies. Who the heck is Perry Grand, anyway?"

Janie laughed. "It's Cary Grant," she said slowly, emphasizing the syllables. He's a wonderful actor, and he's cute. North by Northwest is on tonight."

"Oh, I feel so much better. I've never heard of *North by Northwest*. Are you sure that's the name of the movie?"

"Yes, it's a well-known Alfred Hitchcock movie. You've heard of Alfred Hitchcock, right?"

"Yes, I've heard of Alfred Hitchcock. He's the one who makes those scary movies. Right? Why would you want to watch a scary movie when you've got your own scary movie playing right outside your window?"

"Because it will take my mind off what's outside my window. I'm going to go. I think I've got some Ben and Jerry's in the fridge. If Chunky Monkey doesn't help—nothing will."

"Okay, but keep your phone close by and call me if anything happens."

"You know I will. Have a good night and I'll call you in the morning."

Janie went to the kitchen and began scooping up a large bowl of ice cream.

Da-Da, Da-Da. ...

Dropping the ice cream scoop, she grabbed the phone.

"Now what?" she exclaimed, expecting to hear Heather on the other line.

No reply.

"Hello?" The anxious feeling returned.

No answer.

"Is anyone there?" She could hear slow breathing coming through her phone. Someone was there. She checked the screen: Caller Unknown.

"Look, this isn't funny! Is anyone there?"

Breathing.

Janie clicked the phone off.

Reminding herself to breathe, she walked to the window and peeked out at the black truck still parked there. As she watched, the truck came to life. The engine started. The lights flashed on. Slowly, the truck backed out of the parking space, paused as if taking one last look, then drove away.

Janie forgot all about the ice cream.

DEBBIE ANDERSON

5

The wind howled, blowing the limbs of the tree outside her window. Janie thought she heard something outside her apartment door. She strained to hear it over the wind.

There it was again.

A light tapping sound. It came closer. Was it footsteps? Closer and closer. The closer the tapping came, the more certain she was. Footsteps.

Suddenly, the sound stopped. Whomever they belonged to was now directly outside her apartment.

Creeping on tiptoe, she made her way to the door, leaning forward to peer into the peephole. A dark figure dressed head to toe in black was standing on the other side. A mere two inches of wood stood between them.

As she watched, the figure leaned his ear closer. He was listening to her. She gasped, then clasped her hand over her mouth. She looked out the peephole again. He turned and started walking away.

Without warning, the figure turned and lunged at the door. A loud cracking of wood filled the still night as the door gave way.

Janie screamed.

Frantic, she tried to run, but it was too late. A blanket covered her. She felt herself lifted and thrown to the couch. Screaming, Janie fought to find her way out of the heavy cloth. She crashed to the floor, fighting for her freedom.

But she was alone. Janie was lying in between her couch and coffee table. The throw she draped on her couch was now on her head and twisted around her arms and legs.

Da-da, Da-da ...

Janie stared at the phone lying on the floor beside her. She was still breathing hard, trying to wake up, not sure what was a dream and what was reality. She took a deep breath and looked at the screen on her phone.

"Hi, Heather. What are you doing up so early?"

"Early? It's nearly ten o'clock. Don't you have to work today?"

"Ten o'clock? I must have forgotten to turn on my alarm. Yeah, I have to be at work in an hour."

"I won't keep you. I wanted to make sure you were okay after last night."

"I'm fine. Weird dreams are all."

"Yeah, me too. I'll let you get ready for work. I'll talk to you later. Be careful out there."

"I will. Later."

Janie headed for the shower.

That evening, she stepped out of the front doors of the fabric store. She'd spent the day teaching sewing classes and demonstrating the new quilting machines to customers. She loved her job.

Her grandmother taught her to sew on an old treadle machine years ago. Janie helped quilt many of the quilts her grandmother made. She loved the fabric and could spend hours looking around a fabric store. Now she worked in one. Sharing her obsession with other like-minded people didn't seem much like work. Although, she did like getting that paycheck at the end of the week.

She was nearly at her car when she noticed a black truck parked beside it and fought to keep the panic at bay. She decided to keep walking past her car in an attempt not to draw attention to herself.

She pulled out her phone and dialed the store.

The store manager answered, and Janie explained her predicament. She heard an engine rev and watched the truck pull out of the parking place and slowly creep down the parking lot until it was parallel to her.

"I need help quick," she yelled into her phone. "It's following me."

Still holding the phone to her ear, the manager grabbed Tony, her assistant manager, who was walking by. "Janie needs help! She's in the parking lot and someone is following her. Hurry!" The manager pushed Tony toward the door. "I'm calling the police!"

Tony ran to Janie. She was obviously upset. She stood frozen in place on the sidewalk, staring at a black truck that had stopped across from her.

"Are you okay?"

"No." She didn't move her eyes away from the truck.

"Who's that?" he nodded at the truck.

"I don't know. He's been following me."

Tony looked from Janie to the truck and back to Janie.

"Want me to talk to him?"

"No!"

"Want me to walk you to your car?"

"Not while that truck's there." Janie still hadn't moved.

"What if we go back inside?" Tony looked at the truck, then took Janie by the arm to lead her inside. Slowly, she began backing her way to the store door.

"Wouldn't it be faster if we turned around?" Tony stared at the truck, who moved slowly along with them.

"Don't turn your back on him."

The sound of sirens screamed in the distance. The store manager and several customers were standing in front of the store watching Janie, Tony, and the truck.

As the sirens got closer, the truck revved his engine twice, then slowly drove to the exit.

"Get the license plate number," Janie

shouted.

"There is no license plate," Tony replied.

Two police cars pulled into the parking lot. Relieved, Janie glanced at the squad cars, then looked for the truck.

It was gone.

DEBBIE ANDERSON

6

Flashing red and blue lights illuminated the area with an eerie cast causing all those in the parking lot to feel the tension of the evening, even though they may not know why. Many came forward to give statements to the police; others stood by and watched.

Janie's manager took her inside the store so she could sit down in the back room. She took deep, measured breaths, concentrating on her breathing to slow her galloping heart.

"What happened?" asked the manager. "You scared me to death."

"He fo-followed me." Janie stammered.

"Who?"

"The man in the black truck."

The manager frowned and got a cold bottle of water out of the refrigerator, offering it to Janie.

"Start from the beginning and tell me what happened. Now, who's following you?"

Janie took a sip of water and another deep breath. "A man driving a black truck with dark-tinted windows has been following me. Tonight, he parked right beside my car. I saw him and kept walking, hoping he didn't spot me before I could get help, but I didn't make it. He started following beside me as I walked. Tony saw it."

The manager's eyes were wide as she listened to the story. "Who is it?"

"I don't know!"

"But you know it's a man."

Janie inhaled as she realized it could be a woman. "No. Not really. I just assumed it was a man. What kind of woman would do something like that?"

"There' are a lot of crazy women out there," the manager reminded her. "How long has this been going on?"

"Just since yesterday. It followed me home from dinner last night, parked in the parking lot outside my apartment and just sat there for a long time."

"How did he know you work here? Maybe it was someone else."

"It was the same truck. I don't know how he knew unless he followed me." Janie took another sip of water, wrapping her arms around herself.

The manager patted Janie on the head like a puppy. "I'm sure it will be fine. He's probably just trying to scare you."

"Well, he succeeded."

One police officer stepped into the room. He suggested the manager give her statement to the officer waiting in another room.

The officer took a seat across the table from Janie. He took his time pulling out his notebook and pen. He scanned the notes he had already taken.

He raised his head, looked at Janie with a smile, and began his questioning. "Now, Ms. Alexander, we've gotten statements from most of the witnesses in the parking lot. How about you tell me your version? From what I can tell, you are the main character."

Janie nodded. Taking a deep breath, she began with the phone call from Heather the night before, telling her she was being followed and continued the sequence until the truck followed her in the parking lot here at work. The officer nodded and asked her questions as she went. Finally, he put his pencil behind his ear and looked at her.

"Ms. Alexander, I'm not sure if anyone is actually following you or if it's a figment of your imagination. Based on the statements of the people who witnessed the parking lot incident, I'm inclined to believe you are being followed. That doesn't necessarily mean you're in danger, but it does mean you may be. You're going to have to be careful of your surroundings and call us if you see this truck again.

"I'm going to give you my card. I'll write my home and mobile numbers on the back. If you see or hear anything strange, you call me immediately. If for any reason you can't reach me, leave me a message. I will get right back to you."

Janie nodded to the officer and took his card. "Thank you."

They spoke for a few more minutes as he asked her questions about any strange people or other unusual things that had happened lately. Then he offered to follow her home. She told him she didn't believe it was necessary, but he insisted he would feel better if he knew she got home okay, so she agreed. She would feel better, too.

Janie quickly said goodbye to her co-workers and walked out to her car. The police officer followed. She kept her eyes moving as she watched for the black truck. Dark shadows filled her peripheries, causing her to jump at the slightest breeze. She unlocked her car and climbed in, locking the door behind her. She turned on the ignition. The police officer flashed his lights to let her know he was there and ready to go.

The officer followed her the entire way home. Then he walked her up to her apartment and checked to make sure there were no surprises waiting for her inside. "Everything looks fine, unless you see something out of place."

Janie assured him everything did look fine and thanked him for following her home. "Keep my card nearby. If you need me, call me."

She watched him go to his squad car and waved from the window. She was glad he followed her home, but as soon as he was out of sight, she began to shake.

Peeking between the blinds, she found the parking lot empty of black trucks. Security lights lit up the line of silent vehicles. Satisfied no one was waiting outside, she checked again to make sure she locked the door and windows..

As she picked up the knife from the kitchen counter, she saw the cast-iron skillet that had belonged to her grandmother. "Maybe I can't stab anyone, but surely I could bean them with a frying pan and this one is heavy enough to keep him from getting up again." Grabbing the skillet, she headed for bed, tucking the pan in beside her.

DEBBIE ANDERSON

7

Janie slept fitfully. Nightmares of black trucks with chrome teeth in their grills haunted her sleep. She woke in a tangle of sheets, her head at the foot of her bed. She was tired from two nights of little sleep. Picking her pillows from the floor, she righted herself and pulled the blanket over her head, hoping for a few more hours of sleep.

She was just beginning to doze when her groggy brain registered what day it was. Sunday. She had a date with Shawn. She momentarily considered calling in sick for her date but then remembered she didn't have his number. She pulled a pillow over her head and considered being a no-show, but that was rude. As she lay there, she thought about the handsome cop with the sexy dimples and the cute butt and felt her stomach and lower regions get tingly. She smiled to herself as she tried to picture him naked.

"Whoa, girl! It's too early and you've had too little sleep to be going there."

She really did want to meet Shawn. What better way to get her mind off the chaos that was her life. Besides, he was a police officer. Can't get safer than that.

Tossing the pillow back on the floor and kicking off the covers, Janie climbed out of bed. Her head felt like it was full of feathers and the nasty taste in her mouth confirmed it. She shuffled to the kitchen to start the coffee, then headed for the shower.

An hour later, she was pulling on her best fitting jeans and a V-necked tee shirt. Picking up her cup, she inhaled the hot, aromatic amber liquid. Mmmm - Heaven. She smiled and took a large gulp of the hot-as-lava coffee, burning the roof of her mouth.

Sticking her mouth under the facet, she sucked in cold water. "What are you trying to do, burn the skin off your tongue? Have you forgotten you have a date? Try to French kiss with your lips swollen and peeling."

Sticking out her tongue, she surveyed the damage in the bathroom mirror, determining she would live to kiss another day. She went to the kitchen and dropped an ice cube in the scalding liquid.

One last check in the mirror. Her jeans fit her well and made her butt look good. The soft blue tee skimmed over her curves and hinted at a possibility of cleavage just below the V.. She tossed her head to fluff her long, flaxen, hair and applied a tawny lip-gloss with just a little sparkle. She was ready.

She hesitated for a second before she opened the door. Then, taking a deep breath, she turned the knob and headed out for her date.

Driving to their meeting spot, Janie began to have second thoughts. She knew better than to go out with someone she didn't know. Mentally, she clicked off what she knew about Shawn—

One. He's a cop. That should count for two things, shouldn't it? After all, I couldn't get much safer than dating a police officer!

Two. Uhhh, he has a good sense of humor!

Three. He's good looking.

Four. He has a well-built body, so he can protect me!

Five. That dimple!

She pulled into the parking lot and found a parking place at the far end.

Six. He's a cop! Did I already say that?

Oh, what am I thinking? I don't even know his last name. I didn't tell anyone where I was going! I don't even know where I'm going! I'll call Heather and tell her where I am and who I'm with. If anything happens to me ...

She was about to make the call when a red

Honda Civic pulled up beside her. Too late for a phone call.

She was relieved to see the little car instead of a big, black truck. Then, as Shawn got out of the car, all thoughts of stalkers and trucks evaporated. He was gorgeous! He wore blue jeans that fit perfectly in all the right places. His chocolate brown polo shirt emphasized his broad shoulders and muscular chest. Janie gulped and smiled as he opened her door. She continued to stare at him with a goofy smile as he waited for her to get out.

"Are you ready to go?"

"Sure," she answered and continued to stare at him. He offered his hand to help her out of the car, but his muscular arms distracted her.

"Do you think maybe we should get going?"

Janie blinked, breaking the spell, and forced her eyes away from his biceps.

She took his hand to step out of the car, staring into his eyes as she did. Suddenly, her shoe caught on the doorframe, and she lost her balance, falling right into him.

His powerful arms quickly caught her. "Are you alright?" He was staring down into her eyes. For a minute, she lost her breath. His arms felt strong and protective around her.

Giving her head a quick shake, she regained her composure and stood up. Her face flushed.

"I'm so sorry. I guess my foot caught. How embarrassing!"

"No problem. I liked it." He smiled, his arms still around her. His lips close to hers. He sighed. "I suppose we should get going. I hope you brought comfy walking shoes."

Shawn turned and led her to the passenger door of his Honda. Janie followed.

"I wore these tennis shoes. I hope they'll be okay. I wasn't sure what we were going to be doing." She folded herself into her seat.

"It's a surprise. I am hoping this will be something you enjoy. If not, just say so and we'll go somewhere else."

Yeah right. I still don't know where we're going. If. we're going to a dungeon or somewhere for you to attack me, I'll wish I had my stilettos. Janie flashed a smile. "I'm sure it will be fine. If you like it, I'm sure I will too. Um...we're not going to go fishing, are we?"

Shawn laughed. "No, it's not fishing—but thanks for the heads up! Now, buckle up."

They each put on their seat belts and Shawn headed the car toward a mysterious destination. Minutes later, they were entering the parking lot of Trader Town, a gigantic flea market on the edge of town.

Janie's eyes opened wide and her smile even wider.

"Oh, my."

"Now, like I said, if you don't like it, we can go somewhere else."

"Are you kidding? I love it! I haven't been here in ages."

"Neither have I. I try to make the trip at least

once a year. I thought today would be a good day for it since it's not too hot."

Janie looked at the sky. It was a beautiful day. The sun was warm, but there was a pleasant breeze. Texas in June was unpredictable. It could easily be unbearably hot. But today was exactly right. Janie could hear birds singing. "It's perfect!" She smiled at Shawn, and he took her hand as they headed for the entrance.

8

The sun shone bright and warm. Fluffy clouds frolicked across the sky, chased by a light breeze. They couldn't have ordered a better day for bargain hunting. Janie and Shawn darted from booth to booth, deal to deal, like a couple of butterflies, flitting through a field of wildflowers.

As they walked, Shawn told Janie he liked to refinish furniture. As a child, he helped his father to make ugly pieces into beauties by scraping paint, applying stain, and polishing the wood to restore its natural luster. She could see the passion in his eyes and his body as he became animated, using his hands as he spoke.

Janie shared her love of the same thing, and her enjoyment of finding unusual fabrics and textiles, old quilts, and other hidden treasures.

Janie bought a large tote bag made from recycled burlap coffee bags at one booth to carry small collectables and a vintage tablecloth.

They couldn't resist purchasing a coupled of corny dogs and chomped away as they went.

"The problem I always have is finding someone with a truck, so I can get furniture home. Usually, I just end up with what I can carry. Sometimes I bring a small wagon, which helps, but it's just not big enough for anything large."

Shawn nodded, taking another bite of the corny dog. "I know what you mean. I can't get much in my car. Luckily, I have a friend that I can call if I need to transport something."

He wiped a dab of mustard from the corner of Janie's mouth with his finger and popped the finger in his mouth. "Best mustard I've ever tasted." He smiled his lopsided smile and winked. Janie smiled back.

Without warning, he pulled her close and kissed her. Janie leaned into his broad chest, feeling the warmth of his firm body. He kissed her again. This time with total abandon.

His lips were soft and sweet. His tongue probing. Hungry. Janie kissed him back with the same wanting and urgency. Her brain is a replaying record of want, desire, lust. Give me more, more, more ...

He pulled away just far enough to look into her eyes. A crowd that gathered to watch their embrace clapped. Shawn grinned, planting another peck on her nose. Janie blushed and smiled slightly.

Two twenty-something girls whistled and called, "Hold on to him, honey. He's fine!" Janie nodded and gave them a small wave.

Hand in hand, they continued their search for treasure. Shawn veered toward a dusty, old table. "Don't worry if you find anything big. We'll get it home," Shawn called back to her, never taking his eyes off his prize.

Janie grinned and watched him as he rubbed the surface of the table. He walked around it as if it were the most beautiful thing he had ever seen. As Shawn called the booth owner over to discuss the price, Janie headed for a chest of drawers that needed some work.

She was checking out the dovetailing on the drawers and imagining how she would refinish it, when suddenly she was shoved from behind. Janie bounced off the chest of drawers, skinning her shin and landed in the middle of a bent-wood rocker.

The cane seat had some damage before she fell into it, but now the seat was completely gone, and she was stuck in the middle of it. Her bottom was nearly touching the ground, her knees bent over the front rails, her armpits rested on the back rails. Mustard from her corndog was on her face, her shirt, and her legs but she still had a hold on the stick. Looking around, she realized people were staring at her, others were pointing. Her cheeks burned with embarrassment.

Janie took hold of the rungs and tried to pull herself out of the chair, but she couldn't budge. If only she could get her legs down to the ground. She tried again to pull herself out by her arms. A very unfeminine grunt escaped her mouth, and she remained stuck.

A couple of cowboys walked by, laughing and pointing. "Thanks for your help. You're such gentlemen," she yelled, bringing more attention to her predicament and more laughter from the cowboys.

Finished negotiating, Shawn watched as the owner attached a red, sold sign on top of the table. Engrossed in the purchase, he hadn't taken notice of the surrounding commotion. Now, as he looked for Janie, he was curious as to what was happening. Making his way through the crowd, he was shocked to find Janie stuck in the rocking chair.

"Help." Janie pleaded weakly, seeing Shawn coming toward her. Shawn tried to keep a straight face, but when he realized just how stuck she was, he couldn't help but laugh. He grabbed her under her arms, but she was wedged in too tight. He tried to pull her legs free, but they were immovable.

He stopped and took a step back to evaluate the situation. Taking a fresh look, he broke out in peals of laughter. He was laughing so hard tears ran down his face. The people watching them were laughing too, first at Janie, then at Shawn. Every time he regained his composure, he'd look at Janie and begin a fresh bout of laughter, with the audience following suit.

"Shawn, this is not one bit funny." Janie pushed and pulled at the chair that bound her. "I suggest you get me out of here right now before I lose my sense of humor." One look at her red face told him she had already lost it and he had better find a solution to free her.

One spectator walked closer, scrutinizing the situation. He wasn't laughing. His wife, who apparently pushed her husband forward, remained in the crowd, frowning at those around her.

"Maybe someone should push from underneath, while someone else pulls from on top," the man suggested, rubbing his chin. "Looks like she's in there good."

"I think you might be right. Would you give me a hand?"

"I'll give you both of my hands. Let's get that poor girl out of there."

The good Samaritan got down on his hands and knees to push from below while Shawn grabbed her arms. They heaved and pulled, but nothing happened.

"She's stuck," the man declared. "Maybe if we tip the chair over on its side, we can get to her bottom easier."

Shawn nodded. "Let's try it." Ever so gently, they tipped the rocker and Janie on its side. The man took his position at her bottom while Shawn grabbed her arms. One man pushed while the other pulled. They fought the chair, but the chair hung on.

Red-faced, Janie wanted to tell Shawn to take her home that way. She'd find a way of escape without all the people watching. But Shawn was concentrating on the task at hand, and he wouldn't have heard her, anyway.

"We might have to take the chair apart," Shawn suggested.

The shop owner stepped forward at this suggestion. "If you break it, you buy it," he threatened. "Let me see if I can help get her out of there." The booth owner was a large bear of a man, and the color drained from her cheeks as Janie thought of him pulling on her. *Wonder if there will be anything left of me after this.* She imagined herself as the *Wizard of Oz*

Scarecrow, with parts of her scattered in all directions.

The owner walked around the chair, making his own evaluation. He then nodded and turned to another large man in the crowd. "Come over here and give us a hand."

The new man walked over, and the owner took charge. "Okay, this is what we're going to do—You will push from the bottom, you will pull her arms, I'll pull her legs, and you will hold the chair." There were nods from all involved, as well as the crowd watching. No one was laughing now.

The owner looked at the four men now in position around Janie and said, "Okay, on three—One. Two. Three."

The men pushed, pulled, grunted, and held their breath. Janie grunted and held her breath with them. Nothing happened.

As the men scratched their chins, the wife of the first man from the crowd stepped forward, carrying a pan of cold, cooking grease. "Try this. You just need some lubrication."

"Where in the world did you find grease, Ma?" The man took the container from his wife.

"That nice young fella at the corny dog place gave it to me. It just didn't look like you were going to get her out without it."

"You're probably right. Okay, you all take a handful and let's get her greased up."

Janie felt tears welling up under her eyelids. Hands came from everywhere, slathering her with stinky grease from the fryer.

The owner passed a rag around for the men to remove the grease from their hands, then told everyone to take their places.

"Say a prayer, Ma," called the man.

"Already done, Pa." Janie took a quick glance around. People had their fingers crossed, a boy was rubbing a rabbit's foot, others waved their hands to the heavens.

The four men took their positions. "One. Two. Three." Janie was pushed, pulled, and manhandled again. Sweat poured from their faces. Grunts and groans escaped from their mouths. Then, POP. She burst loose from her captor, sending all four men tumbling. The crowd cheered and clapped. The men smiled, shook hands, and slapped each other on the back. Janie slowly rolled over on her hands and knees.

"Are you okay? Do you need an ambulance?" The woman pulled a hankie out of her purse, spit on it and started wiping mustard and a glob of grease from Janie's face.

"I'm okay. More embarrassed than anything else," Janie whispered.

The woman turned to the crowd. "She's just fine." The crowd cheered again. "I think it's time for everyone to move on now. Let her have some air." The crowd mumbled as they slowly went on their ways.

"Thank you for your help."

"You are welcome. Please be careful. I'd

hate for you to get stuck again."

Janie nodded at her and blushed even more as she inspected the grease stains on her favorite jeans.

The woman collected her husband, who nodded at Janie and smiled. The other man, recruited from the crowd, left without a word, as if pulling a girl from a chair was a daily event. The owner examined the rocker, tsking, and shaking his head at the damage.

"Are you okay?" Shawn asked as he put an arm around Janie's shoulder.

"I am now."

"What happened? You were really stuck."

"Someone pushed me - hard; I lost my balance and landed in the chair."

"Who pushed you?" Shawn scanned the crowd, looking for the guilty party.

"I don't know. I was looking at the chest of drawers and suddenly I was pushed from behind. Somehow, I bounced off the chest and landed in the chair."

Tears rolled down Janie's face. Shawn pulled her to him and wiped the tears with his thumb. "It's okay. I'm just glad you're okay. Are you ready to go?" Janie nodded.

"I bought that table. Did you notice the claw feet? It's going to be beautiful once I clean it up. Did you find anything? You were looking at that chest of drawers. Did you want to get it?"

Janie nodded. "Yeah, it's well made. There's a vintage travel poster I want, too."

Shawn called the owner over and they haggled down the price for the chest of drawers and the poster. Then, at the last minute, Shawn turned back to the owner. "One more thing. How much for the rocker?"

The owner looked at the rocker, then at Janie. "I'll just throw it in with the rest of your stuff. No charge. I think she's already paid enough." He nodded at Janie and shook Shawn's hand to seal the deal. Janie didn't think she could get any redder, but she was wrong.

Once the sold signs were attached to their purchases, Shawn pulled out his cell phone and entered a number. Janie watched as Shawn listened to the ringing.

"Hey Charley. What are you doing?" Shawn listened to the response. "You're kidding me. That's where I am! I was hoping you could bring some furniture home for me."
He listened again. "Okay, I'm going to get my car and bring it up to the front. Can you meet me there in about five minutes? Thanks, Charley."

Shawn looked at Janie, "Charley's here. Can you believe it? Charley's a friend of mine who has a truck. We're going to meet out front in a few minutes so we can load our goodies."

"What a coincidence. That's great. Guess we all thought it was a good day for bargains!" Janie smiled. Shawn put his arm around her shoulder as they walked to the exit.

"I know that whole rocking chair episode wasn't much fun for you. But I really enjoyed being with you today. I had a lot of fun."

"I did too. Right until they pushed me into that rocking chair."

Shawn tried to keep a straight face. "Yeah, that couldn't have been fun. But look at it this way, you sure made a lot of other people happy."

Janie slugged him in the arm. "By the way, why did you buy that rocker?"

"So, I'll always have a reminder of this day." He grabbed her hand before she could punch him again and leaned in for a kiss. The kiss was sweet and soft. Janie felt warm inside and all thoughts of her entrapment faded away.

A few minutes later, they parked along the curb in front Trader Town. "There's Charley now. Why don't you wait here a minute and I'll take care of this?"

Before Janie could say anything, Shawn jumped out of the car and ran toward the back. Janie looked at her greasy clothes. A quick look in the rear-view mirror and she knew she was a mess. She quickly tried to finger-comb her hair as she turned around to see if she should get out and join them.

Behind the car was a black truck with tinted windows. As she watched, the driver's door opened. Someone dressed in a black hoodie and black jeans stepped out. They were tall and lean, but Janie couldn't see their face. Shawn greeted the driver with a hug. They spoke for a few minutes, and Shawn turned back to the car. "Charley's going to take care of it. Is it okay if we bring your stuff over to your place tomorrow?"

Janie gaped at Shawn. She couldn't say anything. There was no way to prove it, but she had a strong feeling that it was the same truck that had been following her? How does Shawn know this guy?

"Janie? Are you okay?"

Janie nodded. "Sure, tomorrow will be fine."

"You don't look so good. You're pale, suddenly. Do you feel okay?"

"I'm fine. I'm just a little tired. Guess that fight with the rocker took it out of me."

"I understand. I'll take you back to your car. Will you be okay to drive?"

Janie assured him she would be fine.

Soon, they pulled up next to her car. Shawn leaned back and looked at Janie. "I really had a good time today. I'd like to take you out again, if that's okay."

"I'd like that." *Unless you are involved with the crazy black truck that has been following me.*

"I'll call you in the morning to make arrangements to deliver your things. I want to hear what you're going to do with that dresser."

"We can talk about it in the morning. I'll make the coffee."

"I'll bring the bagels. Maybe we can eat

them this time." Shawn grinned at her. Janie slugged him in the arm.

9

Janie stood under the hot steamy shower. She had little sleep, unable to turn her brain off from what she had learned the day before. When she did sleep, she had horrible dreams of Shawn, dressed in a black hoodie, laughing with another man, also dressed in black. They chased her with a black truck as she tried to run from them while stuck in a rocking chair. She couldn't move. The chair remaining in the same place, rocking.

She poured citrus shower gel in her hand, breathing in the lemony smell, hoping it would wake her up. The water felt good as it pelted against her skin. The heat messaged her sore muscles, which remembered every second of her imprisonment in that darn rocking chair.

"Who pushed me? It wasn't Shawn. I saw him talking to the shop owner. What about this Charley that just was at Trader Town and drives a black truck?" Janie puzzled over the situation as the sudsy gel rinsed from her body and down the drain.

Minutes later, she was sitting at the breakfast bar with a large steaming mug of rich smelling coffee. Could Shawn be part of this harassment? Could Charley? Obviously, there must be more than one black truck in all of Texas. What if they are involved? Is it safe to tell him where I live?

She remembered the fun they had looking for unique items at the flea market. A smile curled her lips as she thought about it. *Right up until someone pushed me into that rocker.*

"I'm going to tell Shawn I'll come and pick up the dresser. That way he won't know where

I live." Janie felt a second of relief until she remembered he was a cop. Cops have ways of finding people's addresses. *He probably already knows where I live. He has probably been with Charley following me in that darn truck.* The more she thought about it the higher her shoulders rose until they were nearly at her earlobes. She could feel the tension gathering along her spine and shoulders.

Da-da, da-da, ... Janie stared at her phone. *Shawn! What do I do?*

"Answer it, you dummy!"

Picking up the phone, she took a deep breath, "Hello."

"Hey, good-looking. You ready for me to make a delivery?"

"Uhhhh. Yeah, okay."

"Are you sure? You sound kinda hesitant."

"Of course, I'm sure." Janie replied trying to sound more confident.

"Great. Give me your address and I'll head your way."

Janie gave him her address and hung up to wait.

Frazzled, she went to the refrigerator to find something to help soothe the doubts, jumping like frogs in her stomach. She pulled out a large container of *Cool Whip* and grabbed a spoon from the dishwasher. As she scooped the luscious topping into her mouth, she continued to debate the situation with herself.

Shawn probably doesn't know anything about this truck thing. It's probably Charley. But I don't know Charley. Why would he follow me? Oh, heck. Why do I always borrow trouble? It's probably neither of them. Just a coincidence, that's all. She took another big bite of the faux whipped cream and then looked down at the container in horror.

"What are you doing, Janie? People don't just eat whipped topping from the tub."

She returned to the refrigerator, debating about opening the roll of cookie dough or popping the lid on a can of frosting, when her doorbell rang. Janie froze. He's here. She took another large scoop of *Cool Whip* and stuffed it in her mouth before putting the container back in the refrigerator.

Checking her reflection in the mirror by the front door, she wiped a glob of topping from her face and tried to fluff her still-wet hair.

"Good morning," Janie sang as she opened the door, greeting the handsome cop. She quickly stuck her hand out to shake his hand. Shawn frowned and took her hand.

"I thought we had gone past the hand-shaking stage." He pulled her to him and kissed her hard, turning her legs to jelly. He smelled of soap and cologne. Is he wearing *Old Spice*? Janie took a deep breath, inhaling him.

"Shall we get your dresser out of the truck first, or would you rather start with bagels?" He held a bakery bag in front of her, shaking it, teasingly.

"Sure," Janie practically purred.

Shawn gave her a quizzical frown, arching one eyebrow. "Are you sure you're okay?"

"Of course," Janie purred, still thinking about the kiss, then, realizing how she sounded, "I mean, of course."

Shawn grinned. "Then let's do it."

Janie shook her head to herself back to the present. "Do what?" she asked, hesitantly.

Shawn shook his head, "Get your dresser from the truck." He put the bagels on the table and headed for the door, Janie following behind.

"Uh, where's Charley?" she asked.

"Oh, Charley ended up having plans this morning, so I borrowed the truck."

"That's convenient."

She climbed up into the bed of the truck and began pushing the beat-up old dresser toward the tailgate. As Shawn grabbed the other side of the chest, she asked nonchalantly, "So how well do you know Charley?"

Shawn gave her a quizzical look. "I've

known Charley most of my life - since we were kids. We grew up together. Why all the questions about Charley?"

"Oh, no reason" She climbed out of the truck and took her end of dresser. The old chest was heavy and neither of them spoke again as they heaved it across the parking lot.

Back in Janie's apartment, they set the chest down with a thud. Both breathed deeply as they caught their breath.

"So, tell me what you saw in this old thing." Shawn asked as he walked around it, taking in the scratches and peeling paint.

"Are you kidding me? It's beautiful," Janie gushed. Glimpsing Shawn's doubting face, she laughed. "Okay, maybe it's not so beautiful now, but it will be. Wait here, I'll show you."

Janie ran into her bedroom and pulled a large vintage travel poster from her closet. Running back to the living room, she unfurled the poster and held it across the front of the dresser. "See?" She looked at Shawn like this made perfect sense.

"So, you're going to hang a poster in front of it? That is an improvement, but I don't see how it would be very practical. How do you get to the drawers?"

"No, I'm not going to hang the poster in front of it. I guess you will have to wait and see. Trust me; it's going to be beautiful."

"If you say so," Shawn replied, grinning. "By the way, do I smell coffee?"

They headed to Janie's small kitchen. Shawn took a seat at the table while Janie poured the coffee. She placed a mug of the steamy potion in front of him and went back for plates, napkins, and silverware. She opened the bag and started placing the contents on a plate. "Oh, 'everything bagels', my favorite."

"I wasn't sure what kind of bagels you liked. Other than hard ones, you can fling at unsuspecting police officers."

Janie laughed at the memory. "You must admit, it worked. You're here, aren't you?" She gave him a sly smile.

"Oh, I see. It was all part of your plan to seduce me and get me into your lair."

"Like I said, it worked, didn't it?"

Shawn reached across the table and took her hand. "How do you know it wasn't my plan?"

"What, you planned for me to toss a bagel out of my window so you could pull me over?"

"No, I was just trying to find an excuse to stop you. You are pretty cute."

"You're pretty cute yourself," Janie replied.

Suddenly, Shawn pulled his hand away. "Oh, I almost forgot. I didn't just bring bagels. Opening a second bag, he pulled out two huge, cream-filled donuts. These were screaming at me from the display case—I had to get them."

"Hate it when that happens." Janie's stomach gave a flip as she remembered the whipped topping she had eaten earlier. Eating anything with cream filling did not tempt her in the least.

The couple munched on bagels and sipped coffee as they conversed about the wonderful treasures they had found at Trader Town.

"It's just a shame you got yourself stuck in the rocking chair," Shawn commented with a mischievous grin. "Or was that part of your plan, too?"

"Yeah, right." Janie quipped as she slugged him in the arm.

"You must admit, it was strange. Tell me again how it happened."

"Someone pushed me. I told you, I was looking at the dresser, you know, really concentrating on how well it was made. I guess I must have been bent down slightly, checking out the drawers. All at once, I felt someone push me hard from behind. I guess I must have bounced off the dresser, tripped over something else, and fallen into the rocker."

Shawn tried to keep a straight face as he listened to her explanation. Suddenly, he spit coffee across the table and roared with laughter. "I wish you could have seen yourself. I'll never forget the vision of you trapped in that chair." By now, he had tears streaming down his face. "Of course, I won't have to." He pulled out his cell phone, pushed a few buttons, and slid his finger across the screen a few times. Then he held up the phone for Janie to see. There in front of her was a picture of her, stuck in the chair. Legs up, armpits around the frame, and butt hanging down below her.

"You didn't!" she screamed, grabbing the phone.

"I did." Shawn jerked the phone out of Janie's reach.

Janie jumped up and crawled up on his chair, standing in Shawn's lap. Somehow, he kept the phone away from her while his other hand began snaking in under her shirt. With this surprise attack, Janie gave a shriek, and lost her balance, landing in Shawn's lap. Taking full advantage of this development, Shawn pulled her close and kissed her.

10

Janie walked Shawn to the black truck and waved as he drove away. She assumed he waved back. The dark windows prevented her from seeing him. A sick feeling settled in her stomach as she considered the possibility of Shawn being involved in stalking her with that truck. Who was this Charley person? Shawn said he was a family friend. Why would he want to stalk her?

Taking a deep breath, she went back to her apartment, picked up her phone, and dialed.

"Hello."

"Heather, what are you doing tonight?"

"Not much. I planned to clean my bathroom and pay some bills."

"Could I convince you to go to Sadie's for a burger?"

"If you twist my arm, I'd even agree to a beer."

"Good. I really need to talk to you."

"Okay. What time?"

"I'd say now, but it's awfully early."

"Now sounds perfect. Besides, if we make it later, I'd have time to clean my bathroom before we go. Believe me, we don't want that to happen."

"I'm sure there is a problem with that logic, but I'm not going to argue. Say fifteen minutes?"

"I'll be there."

Janie picked up her keys and headed out. Heather knew Janie better than anyone. She also had an uncanny way of looking at things logically and telling Janie if she's making something out of nothing.

Minutes later, the two friends were in their favorite booth ordering greasy Sadie Burgers with all the fixings, their favorite go to when things got tough, or when they needed an excuse to eat something fattening.

"So, what's up? Is that truck still following you?"

"Yeah, it's still around. But there's been a recent development."

"Here's to new developments," replied Heather, lifting her beer mug in a toast.

Janie clicked her own mug against Heather's and they both took a long swig.

"I think Shawn might be involved with the truck stalking me."

"What?"

"Yeah, I know. He seems like such a great guy, but he either is my stalker or somehow knows who is."

"Okay. Tell me the whole story. I need to hear this."

Janie started with the trip to Trader Town, the push that landed her in the rocking chair, and the black truck that belonged to Charley. As she spoke, Heather chewed on her burger. Her eyes fixed on Janie. Heather listened without interruption until Janie ended with Shawn borrowing the truck this morning and coming to her apartment.

"I know. I'm probably being paranoid, right? There are lots of black trucks with tinted windows out there. Right? Shawn probably doesn't have anything to do with this."

"You may be paranoid, but you are justified to feel that way," Heather responded, dabbing grease from her mouth and chin. "Did you ask him about it?"

"No. I didn't want to chase him away. I did ask about Charley, but Shawn says he's just a family friend. But why would a family friend follow me unless Shawn asked him to? Oh, I don't know what to do. I really like Shawn."

"I don't know Janie; you haven't known

Shawn long, and the truck didn't follow you until after you met him. Seems like quite a coincidence. You have to confront him. He may be good-looking but so was Ted Bundy."

Janie nearly dropped her beer. "You would mention that. I don't believe Shawn is anything like Mr. Bundy! He's so sweet."

"So was Bundy. Everyone liked him. But he still murdered hundreds of girls."

"Okay, now you're exaggerating. Forget about Bundy, and let's get back to Shawn. He's a police officer. He's paid to serve and protect. Cops don't stalk people."

"Oh, no? What about Drew Peterson? He killed two of his wives. They can't even find one of them. Or Dan Heirs? He molested a little girl and then killed her mother. He was a 'friend of the family', too."

"Okay, stop. I get your point. I need more information about Shawn and this Charley guy."

"Janie, I'm really worried about you. Do not

be alone with either one of them. You just don't know what could happen."

"I know you're right," Janie said disappointedly. "I really like this guy. It's going to be hard to date him if I can't be alone with him."

"Just until we find out more about him. He maybe everything he seems, but we can't be sure, and it's not worth your life if he isn't."

"I know. Let's find out who this Charley is and if Shawn is involved."

"Meanwhile, let's have another beer and tell me again about getting stuck in that chair. I wish I had a picture of that." Heather motioned for the server while Janie told her about the rocking chair incident, this time with more details. The girls laughed and sipped their beers.

Eventually, the humor died away and Janie's strange situation hung soberly over them like a dark blanket.

"I'm going to go," Janie said with

resignation. "I can't think about this anymore. Maybe there's a good movie on Netflix. I'm ready to veg out on the couch for a while. I'll think about the black truck tomorrow."

"Tomorrow is another day," Heather quoted from *Gone With The Wind*. "Just be careful and keep me up to date."

The girls paid their bill and started for the door. Suddenly, Janie came to a stop, causing Heather to run into her from behind. She was staring ahead, the color draining from her face.

"What is it?"

Janie pointed to a booth with several people laughing and clinking beer mugs.

"That's Shawn."

"Which one?"

"The good-looking one with the blonde hanging on his arm."

"Well, he is good-looking. Let's see who she is. You can introduce him to me."

Janie nodded, lifted her head high, and marched with purpose toward the table.

Heather followed behind, trying to keep up. Just as Janie reached the booth, Shawn turned and saw her. He smiled and started to stand to greet her.

"Don't get up. We're not staying. I just wanted to say hello before we left."

"Why don't you join us for a while?" Shawn asked. He seemed glad to see her.

"Looks like you're having fun with your friends," Janie stated matter-of-factly. Her eyes narrowed, and her mouth set into a straight line as she stared at the blonde girl still attached to Shawn's arm.

Shawn looked at the blonde and removed her hand. "Let me introduce you to the gang." He went around the booth, introducing the group, ending with the good-looking, blonde-haired person. "And this is Charley."

"Charley? The Charley? The black truck Charley?"

Shawn chuckled, "Yeah. That Charley. I told you we grew up together. She's almost a member of the family."

"Yeah, almost," Charley stated, lifting her chin and looping her arm around Shawn's. She had a defiant attitude, as if she was defending her property.

Janie stared at the beautiful girl with large blue-green eyes, a cute turned-up nose, and a luscious bow-shaped mouth, shiny with a rose-colored lip-gloss. Her long blonde hair was nearly white and framed her perfectly tanned face. Janie noticed this girl Charley was staring at her and quickly looked away.

"You didn't tell me Charley was a girl."

"I guess I didn't think about it. I don't think of her that way. Like I said, we grew up together. She's just part of the gang who just happens to be a girl." Shawn explained.

Janie nodded, looking back at Charley.

Heather stepped forward, introducing herself. She extended her hand for a handshake.

"Oh, I'm sorry. I forgot my manners." Janie

stammered. "This is Heather, my best friend. We grew up together, too."

"Please join us." Shawn scooted over to make room in the booth; his friends did the same. Heather started to sit down next to an attractive guy sitting across from Shawn. Janie grabbed her arm.

"Thank you, but we've got to go," Janie replied. "I'm sure I'll see you soon. Nice to meet you." She glanced around the table and smiled.

"Yes, nice to meet you," Heather added as Janie pulled her away from the booth.

As they stepped out the door, Heather pulled her arm away. "Why didn't we join them for a while? That one friend of Shawn's was good-looking. So was Shawn, by the way. He really wanted you to stay."

"Did you see that girl?"

"Charley?"

"Yeah, Charley. Don't you think it's strange he's never mentioned Charley was a girl? Did you see how she hung on him? He didn't seem to mind."

"Come on Janie. He told you she was just a friend. He probably thinks of her as a kid sister."

"How many guys let their sisters hang on them like that?"

"Okay, so she's kind of possessive. That doesn't mean he feels the same way."

"Kind of? She certainly did not like me. Did you see how she stared at me?"

"Yeah. I also saw how you stared at her. Oh Janie, let it go. She doesn't mean anything to Shawn. Did you see his eyes? He is totally into you. He didn't see anyone but you."

"I don't know. Maybe. I just don't get this Charley thing."

Heather looked at her friend. "You are just overwhelmed with everything. Time to go home, get your jammies on, and watch a good movie. Forget all this for a while. Tomorrow it will make more sense."

"You're right. Do you want to come? I have butter-pecan ice cream and we can pop some popcorn. Lots of butter."

"You've convinced me. Let's go."

11

Janie removed the bag of popcorn from the microwave. Tearing it open, she released the hot, steamy aroma of Orville Redenbacher's best. The buttery smell filled the room, temporarily chasing away the confusion and unpleasantness of the interaction with Shawn and Charley.

Heather scooped another glob of butter pecan ice cream from the container and popped it into a bowl.

"I hope you have chocolate syrup; I'm really craving chocolate syrup with this butter pecan. Or, better yet, some hot fudge." She pulled open the refrigerator door, searching for chocolate.

"It's in the door, the second shelf," Janie instructed.

Finding the jar of hot fudge sauce, Heather unscrewed the lid and turned to warm it in the microwave. "Okay, so tell me what is going on with you and Shawn. And remind me who this Charley is. I thought Charley was the guy following you with the black truck."

"It is!" Janie dumped the popcorn into a large bowl. "But now I find out Charley is a girl! I don't know what to think. Could she be the one who's been following me?" Janie contemplated adding more butter to the Lots of Butter popcorn. Deciding against it, she slammed the bowl on the counter, causing Heather to jump and spill the hot fudge. "Why was she hanging all over Shawn? Do you think they have something going on?"

Heather picked up the two bowls of ice cream and headed for the couch. "I don't know what to think. She was really hanging on him, but he didn't seem to be paying attention to her. He said he didn't think of her as a girl. Is that possible?"

"Are you kidding? She's gorgeous."

Janie picked up the popcorn and a roll of paper towels and followed Heather to the couch.

"Yeah. I must admit, I was kinda crushing on her myself."

Janie glared at Heather.

"Just kidding." Heather put her hands up in surrender. "I think you're going to have to trust Shawn when he says he's not interested. After all, it's you he's going out with, right?"

"I guess. I just don't get what he sees in me when he could obviously have her."

"I don't get it either." Heather said, putting a large spoonful of ice cream in her mouth.

"Thanks a lot." Janie threw a piece of popcorn, which landed in Heather's shiny brown locks.

"I didn't mean it like that. I guess I'm trying to wrap my head around the idea of her stalking you. Do you really think it was her?"

"I keep saying there must be more than one black truck with tinted windows around here. Maybe it's not her. But it is strange the way she just happens to have a black truck, and she just happened to be at Trader Town, and she just happens to be comfortable hanging all over Shawn." Janie popped a kernel of corn in her mouth and picked up her bowl of ice cream.

"That's too many 'just happens to' for me." Heather rolled her eyes. "I think you are going to have to talk to Shawn."

"Yeah, I guess you're right. I just don't want Shawn to think I'm bonkers. What if I'm imagining things? Worse yet, what if he thinks I'm getting all possessive? After all, we've only had one actual date."

"No, I'd count his delivering your dresser as date two.

"Besides, you did have coffee with him at Starbucks, which makes date three." Heather wiggled three fingers at Janie. "Girl, you're practically engaged."

Janie gave her a sarcastic smile. "My head hurts."

"Ice cream rush?"

"No, just too much to think about." Janie rubbed her temples and took a sip of her diet Coke. "Let's watch a movie and think of something else for a while."

While Janie looked for a movie, Heather walked to the window. "It sure is a pretty night. Lots of stars. I love this time of year. It's warm, not too hot, it doesn't get dark until late, and the flowers are blooming. Have you seen the pink ones in front of Mrs. Jenkins house? They smell …"

Janie looked up to see what had stopped Heather's poetic revelry. What she saw sent a chill down her spine. The color had drained from Heather's face and she was backing slowly away from the window.

"What is it?" Janie asked as she ran to the window to see for herself.

"It's out there," Heather whispered, grabbing Janie's arm, but not taking her eyes from whatever she saw outside.

"What?" Janie whispered back.

"The black truck."

Both girls dropped to the floor to keep from being seen. Janie crawled to the lamp, switching it off. Inching forward on hands and knees, they crawled back to the window and peered over the sill. There, parked directly across from her apartment, was a black truck with tinted windows.

The friends lowered themselves below the sill and stared at each other. Their faces, lit only by the television screen, had a ghastly pallor, making the situation even more frightening. Bit by bit, they raised themselves to see over the windowsill again. The truck was still there, even though they had hoped it was a figment of their imaginations.

"What do we do now?" Heather's voice was so low Janie could barely hear it.

Suddenly, Janie stood up. "I'm going out there."

"What?"

"You heard me. It's just Charley, right? It's time to take a stand. I'm not going to be afraid of a weird girl who's trying to scare me, even if she is prettier than me."

"You're much prettier than she is." Heather replied with a certain amount of vibrato. "You're right; it is time to confront her. I'll wait here and watch from the window. If things get ugly, I'll call the police."

"Oh, no you don't. You're coming with me." Janie grabbed Heather's arm and headed for the door.

Seconds later, the two friends were pounding on the door to the truck.

"Open up, Charley. We need to talk," shouted Janie.

"Go away," replied a feminine voice. "I'm not doing anything."

"We just want to talk," Janie replied.

Slowly, the door creaked open. A very frightened Charley looked out at Janie and Heather. "What do you want?"

"What are you doing in my parking lot?" Janie yelled.

"Nothing. It's a free country, isn't it" Charley didn't sound convincing. Janie squinted her eyes and glared at her.

"Oh, okay. I just wanted to see what kind of girl you are. Shawn talks about you all the time. He's interested in you, and I wondered why." Charley's shoulders slumped. She looked miserable.

"Why do you care?"

"I've known Shawn since I was a kid. I've always had a bit of a crush on him. I know he's not interested in me. I just wondered what he saw in you." Charley was staring at the ground and her cheeks flushed.

Janie watched Charley for a few minutes. She looked miserable. "I wonder the same thing." Feeling compassion for the girl, Janie shoved her hand out. "Hi, I'm Janie and this is my friend, Heather. It's nice to meet you. Would you like to join us for a movie? We've got ice cream and popcorn."

Charley slowly raised her eyes to meet Janie's. "Really? You want me to join you?"

"Of course. We can never have enough friends, right?"

Charley smiled, revealing beautiful white teeth between her perfectly formed pink lips. "I guess not. What kind of ice cream?"

Hours later, the three girls were laughing and telling stories. Charley told tales about Shawn from when he was a boy. She admitted that Shawn had always treated her like a little sister and had never been interested in her. She also admitted that she had looked at him as a big brother rather than a boyfriend, even though she liked to think of him that way.

However, when Janie started talking about how scared she had been while Charley followed her, Charley stopped her. "Janie, I have never followed you except tonight."

Charley looked serious.

"Ah, come on. The gigs up." Janie laughed.

"I'm serious," Charley responded. "I haven't been following you."

Janie's smile faded. She looked at Heather and then back at Charley. "But you were at Trader Town last Sunday. Shawn told me you were."

"Yeah, I was there, but I didn't know you and Shawn were until he called to see if I could help pick up his stuff."

"You knew. You pushed me into that rocking chair."

Charley was shaking her head. "No. It wasn't me. Shawn told me about it, but I thought he was making it up. You really were stuck in the rocking chair?"

Heather's eyes were wide as she followed

the conversation, moving her head back and forth between the two girls as if she were watching a tennis match.

"If it wasn't you, then who's been following me?"

The three girls stared at each other. No one had the answer.

"I knew there had to be more than one black truck with tinted windows," Janie whined in frustration.

"I think it's time you spoke with Shawn," Heather spoke with authority. "He needs to know about this."

"I agree." Charley nodded her head. "This isn't something to mess with. Shawn is a cop. He might know what to do."

"Okay. I suppose you're right. I'll talk to him tomorrow."

"Meanwhile, I'm beat. I better be heading home before I fall asleep behind the wheel." Heather yawned to make her point.

"Me too." Charley picked up the empty

dishes and headed for the sink. "Thank you for inviting me in. Just so you know, I approve of you seeing Shawn. He's really a nice guy. And if I can't have him, I guess you should." Charley smiled and gave Janie a hug.

"Well, if it doesn't work out with Shawn, I hope you'll still be my friend."

"What about me?" Heather pretended to be left out.

All three girls laughed as they walked out to the parking lot arm in arm.

"Be careful going home," Janie called as she waved to them. "Watch out for big black trucks." Then, as her two friends, one old and one new, pulled out of the parking lot, Janie headed back to her apartment.

12

Janie ran across the parking lot, sloshing her Grande Cappuccino all over her hand. She stopped at the front door of the fabric store, digging for a napkin in her oversized bag.

"Da, Da. Da, Da. ..."

"Hello."

"Hey, Sunshine." Janie grinned, loving the corniness of Shawn's greeting. "Just thinking about you. I hear you met Charley. She really likes you."

"I like her too. She fits right in with my friends."

"Good to know. She's a good kid."

"Yeah, but she's been told to keep her hands off you," she teased.

"Good luck with that. I've been trying to break her of that habit for a long time."

"So many women - so little time."

"Maybe so, but don't include Charley in that category. She's just a punk kid. A real pest."

"Oh, poor guy. Having to put up with a beautiful woman hanging on you."

"Okay, okay. I guess you're right. She's grown up into a pretty girl."

"Yeah. Now forget about that and go back to thinking of her as a punk kid."

Shawn laughed. "I'll try. But now that you've got me noticing, I may have to rethink my stand on her."

"I don't think so," Janie replied, laughing.

"Um, Janie, the real reason I called was because Charley told me about the truck that's been following you."

"Oh, that."

"Yeah, that. Why didn't you tell me sooner?

This isn't something to mess around with. Whoever this is could be dangerous."

Janie stopped for a second before continuing. "Don't you think it could have been Charley? I know she said it wasn't her, but maybe she was just embarrassed."

"No, I don't think it was Charley. I've known her for a long time. She would have admitted it, if it was her. If not to you, definitely to me."

Janie was silent. Her heart was beating faster thinking about the possibility.

"Janie, are you there?"

"I'm here. What should I do?"

"Let me think about this. Did you get a license plate number?"

"No, the truck didn't have a license plate."

"How many times have you noticed it?"

"I don't know. Several times."

"Okay, I've got to work tonight, so let me think about this and I'll get back to you tomorrow. Meanwhile, lock your door, both your house and car. Have someone walk you to your car tonight. When you get home, check the area before you get out of the car. If you see the truck, don't get out. Instead, you come straight to the police station. Then call me."

"Yes, sir." Janie tried to make light of the situation but wasn't successful.

"I mean it, Janie. I know it's easy to believe nothing will happen to you and you're probably right, but there is always that one chance. I don't want anything to happen to you."

Janie swallowed the lump that was forming in her throat. "I know you're right. I promise I'll be careful, but please call me in the morning so we can discuss how to fix this situation."

"I will. I've got to go. Remember to lock your doors and I'll call you in the morning. If you need me before then, call me."

"Can I call you for anything?" Janie tried to sound enticing but didn't quite make it.

"Absolutely. See ya soon."

"Yeah, soon." Janie listened while the line went dead.

***

Once she returned home, Janie locked the doors to her apartment and plopped onto her sofa. She had replayed her conversation with Shawn several times in her head, worrying herself into exhaustion.

Forcing herself to her feet, she shuffled to the kitchen to find something cold to drink. The heat from the day was still hanging on, even though it was after nine o'clock. She was hot and tired. She considered fixing dinner but changed her mind and settled for ice cream. Janie scooped her bowl full of chocolate almond, poured on extra chocolate syrup, and added a handful of peanuts.

She headed back to the couch, bowl in one hand, with plans for an hour or so of television. On the way, she walked past the window and closed the blinds. She plunked herself down and picked up the remote. Checking *TCM,* she found *Sorry Wrong Number* was just starting. She dug her spoon into the bowl and took a bite of frozen chocolate indulgence. Just what she needed to take her mind off black trucks.

She woke to see a man dressed in black, walking toward Barbara Stanwick. Barbara screamed, and the screen camera moved to the open terrace doors and the sounds of the night beyond. Janie had missed the whole movie. Her bowl was empty, even though she didn't remember anything beyond that first bite. "Guess I was really tired." She stretched, picked up her bowl, and headed to the sink. She rinsed the bowl and yawned.

Checking her watch, Janie saw it was midnight. She stretched again and started to go to bed. One more check of the locks on the door. Then she checked the parking lot. She reached to turn out the light and stopped. Was it out there? Rubbing her eyes, she took one more look.

Suddenly, she wasn't tired anymore. There, sitting directly across from her apartment, was the black truck with tinted windows. She dropped the blind back into place and turned out the light. *What should I do?* She walked back to the door, checking the locks again. Locked.

"Okay, breathe. The doors and windows are locked. No one can get in. You are safe." She bent over taking deep breaths, trying to slow down her racing heart."

Janie tiptoed back to the window, afraid to make any noise. Her hands shook as she lifted the blind and peeked out. Everything was quiet outside. The moon was bright and illuminated the whole parking lot, giving the truck an ominous look and filling her with dread.

"Forget about it and go to bed," she told herself. "Tomorrow you can tell Shawn and let him take care of it."

She couldn't bring herself away from the window, her sight glued to the ominous truck. "What does he want?" The night was still, eerily so. No sound, no people, no wind. She shuttered. "Who is it? Why is he stalking me?"

For a moment, she considered Charley. Charley was sitting in her truck outside the apartment last night. Could it be her?

Janie shook her head, disgusted that she would even consider it. Charley was sweet. She wouldn't hurt a fly. If not her, who?

Janie scanned her brain for any possibility. The man at the grocery store the other day. He seemed to be following her with his shopping cart. At one point, he had run into her. Janie remembered how red he had turned as he apologized. He said he was looking for something and didn't realize she had stopped. Could it be him?

Or, what about the grounds keeper? What was his name? He always smiled and nodded when he saw her. Of course, he was always working, blowing grass clippings, or trimming the bushes. Could that be a ploy? A ruse so he could get closer? What was his name? Dirt? No, Derk. Her mind conjured up his sharp, straight nose, dark busy brows, and his soft smile, and his respectful nod. No, it couldn't be him.

Her new neighbor seemed very aloof. Was that his way of keeping her off track?

Old Mr. Metzger was a little too friendly. He always spoke a little too loud and told those awful jokes - and he always touched her arm or her shoulder when he told the punch line. Him?

Shawn. What did she really know about Shawn? He seemed wonderful, but was he? So many serial killers seemed wonderful right until they killed their victims. But she really did like Shawn. He was good-looking, fun, and boy, could he kiss. It couldn't be him. But Janie knew it could be.

She searched harder for possibilities. She ended up back with Charley. Charley seemed so nice. They had so much fun together the other night. But she did admit to having a crush on Shawn. Maybe it was more?

"I don't really have any reason to suspect anyone. Who is it?"

Janie's was feeling overwhelmed as one by one every person she knew or didn't know became a suspect.

She was still glaring at the truck when a sudden chill filled her with dread. Keeping her eyes on the window, she backed away, letting the blinds fall back into place. Her concrete blocks, previously known as feet, moved too slowly, then stopped, planting her a few feet from the ominous window. Janie continued to stare at the now blocked view, shivering as if a winter gale had just blown through her apartment.

The truck had just flashed its lights at her.

13

Janie took another step back. The truck had flashed its lights. *What does he want?* She shivered just thinking about it. *Obviously, he doesn't care that I know he's out there. He must feel safe.* Grabbing her phone from the table, she dialed Shawn.

"Hello."

"Shawn, it's Janie."

"What's wrong? Are you okay?"

"I'm okay, but that truck is out in the parking lot again. He just flashed his lights at me."

"Are you sure he flashed them at you?"

"Who else is there to flash them at? Yes, he

flashed them at me," Janie screamed.

"Okay, okay. I believe you. Is he still out there?"

"I think so. Hold on." Janie switched off the lamp and moved back to the window. Her fingers trembled as she parted the slats of the blinds and then dropped them as if they were on fire. "Yes, he's still there."

"Janie, I'm on my way. Meanwhile, check your doors and stay away from the window. Do you want me to stay on the line until I get there?"

"No. Just hurry." She tried to sound brave, but her voice came out two octaves higher than normal. Janie released the call and sat the phone on the table. She wrapped her arms around herself and paced back and forth across the living room. Before long, she realized she was gravitating back to the window. Doing a quick U-turn, she headed to the kitchen for a glass of water.

The water was icy and felt good as it made

its way down her throat. She gulped the liquid as if she hadn't had anything to drink for days. Finished, she sat the glass on the counter and wiped her mouth with her hand. She knew she wasn't thirsty; she was scared and needed to take her mind off the parking lot. The water had helped for the moment, but now her stomach was sloshing with a sick nervousness.

Janie took a deep breath and held it. She slowly blew it out, trying to calm herself.

"The doors are locked. Shawn is on his way. Just stay away from the windows. You'll be fine." Taking another deep breath, she headed back to the window, tiptoeing as she went. She watched as her fingers made their way back to the blinds and, with the skill of a surgeon, separated them.

The dark truck sat in the parking lot, daring her to do anything about it. "That's right. Just sit there all smug. You think you've got me where you want me, don't you?" Janie narrowed her eyes and lifted her chin at the truck, trying to act as if it didn't bother her. "Just wait until Shawn gets here, then we'll see who's ..." Janie dropped the blinds and jumped back away from the window.

"Where's Shawn? What's taking him so long?"

Gathering all her courage, she went back to the window. The truck door was open. The lights were on. There, in front of the truck, stood a dark figure dressed head to toe in black. He wore a stocking hat that covered his face. The lights from the truck created an aura around him, making him seem even more sinister. He was staring straight at her.

Janie screamed but could not move. As she watched, he made a 'V' with his fingers and pointed first to his eyes and then to her. He was letting her know he was watching her. Janie stood glued to the spot. Her fingers holding the blinds open. She was terrified.

After what seemed like hours, she let go of the blinds and stepped away from the window. She ran to the door to check the locks again. Locked. Then she ran to the kitchen, pulling out her cast-iron skillet. She was going to protect herself. After a moment, she grabbed a knife from the butcher block on her counter. *Just in case he gets the frying pan away from me.* She took another trembling breath and went back to the living room with her weapons.

She looked around, trying to decide what to do next. Maybe a movie will take my mind off him until Shawn gets here. What is taking him so long? Glancing at her watch, she realized it had only been four minutes since she had spoken to Shawn. She crawled onto the couch and pulled a comforter around her, then picked up the remote and started flipping through channels. Before long she found *When a Stranger Calls*.

It had been a long time since she had watched this movie. She tried to remember when she watched it last and decided it was when she was still living at home. She had watched it with her father. She loved to watch old movies with her father. He's the one that introduced them to her.

She especially enjoyed being scared by horror movies. Of course, she always knew Dad was close by, so she was safe. No monsters would get her. She smiled to herself, picturing the two of them cuddled up on the couch. Her father would pretend to be scared and she would laugh. She realized he did that to dispel her fears.

She began to relax as she watched the film. The babysitter answered the phone, but no one was there. The babysitter went back to her homework. The phone rang again. No answer. The phone rang once more. 'Have you checked on the children?'

Janie felt a chill go up her spine. She gripped the knife in her fingers. The babysitter went to the kitchen. "Don't go in the kitchen,"

Janie yelled at the television.

The phone rang again. 'Have you checked on the children?'

The babysitter calls the police. They are going to listen to her calls. She should keep him on the phone as long as she can, so they can trace the call.

The phone rings again.

Janie leans forward, watching the babysitter try to keep the caller on the line.

'Have you checked on the children?' The caller disconnects.

The babysitter starts up the stairs to check on the children, but just as she gets to the top stair, the phone rings again.

Janie is standing now. "Don't answer it." But the babysitter answers the phone.

The babysitter yells to the caller, 'Leave me alone!'

This time it's the police calling. 'The calls are coming from inside the house. Get out now!'

Janie has moved to stand in front of the television. "Run, run," she shouts.

Da-da, Da-da, ... Janie screams, then realizes it's her phone ringing. "Hello," she shouts into the phone.

"Janie. Are you okay?"

"Yes, I'm okay," she shouted. Then, calming down slightly, she repeats, "I'm okay. Where are you?"

"I'm in the parking lot, but there's no black truck here."

"What?" Janie went to the window and peered between the blinds. No truck. Just Shawn.

"It was there. I promise."

"I believe you. I'm coming in and you can tell me all about it."

Seconds later, Janie opened the door for Shawn. She threw her arms around him, relieved that he was there.

"I guess you're glad to see me." Shawn gave her a hug, then gently pushed her back, so he could look at her. He frowned as he saw the tension on her forehead. Her eyes were wide, and her hands were shaking. "Let's sit down and you can tell me all about it." Taking her hand, he led her to the couch.

He sat down, but quickly jumped back up. Pulling the comforter back, he discovered the frying pan and the knife.

"Been cooking on the couch?" He asked, trying to hide a grin.

"No. I was trying to be safe." Janie responded defensively.

Shawn moved the weapons to the coffee table and sat down again. "Okay, now tell me everything that has happened."

Janie reported all the truck's actions. Shawn stopped her from time to time to ask questions. When she finished, Janie was exhausted. The adrenaline rush she had experienced through the night was subsiding. She felt safe with Shawn there.

"Do you want some coffee? I'm sure you're

tired. I'll make a quick pot." Janie started for the kitchen.

"I don't want any coffee. It's late and it will keep me awake if I drink it now. I think you could use some sleep yourself."

"You're right. Tea then. Do you want regular black tea, or would you prefer chamomile or Sleepy Time? I think I'll have Sleepy Time. How about you?" Janie put the kettle on and turned on the burner.

Shawn followed her to the kitchen. "Janie, I know you've been through an ordeal tonight. But you're safe now. You kept your doors locked and didn't let it get to you. I'm proud of you. Do you really want tea?"

Janie turned to Shawn. "Yes, I really want tea. I need to keep busy for a while so I can calm down."

Shawn pulled Janie close and kissed her. Janie draped her arms around his neck and leaned in closer. As they kissed, their desire for each other grew from a smoldering ember to a forest fire, devouring all fear and hesitation. Shawn pushed her against the kitchen wall and began to make his way down her throat. His kisses burned with lust and desire. Janie surrendered to his heat. She could not get enough of him.

A shrill scream startled them both. They turned toward the sound, realizing the kettle had just whistled. Janie moved the kettle off the burner and turned back to Shawn.

"Are you sure you want tea?" he whispered, pulling her back into his arms.

She answered by wrapping her arms back around his neck, "No. I don't want tea after all."

He smiled down at her, then pulled her in under his chin, holding her close. "I should head for home. It's getting late."

"Yeah, you probably should. Do you have to work tomorrow?" Janie inquired, purring into his neck.

"No, I'm off tomorrow," Shawn responded, pulling her still closer.

"So am I."

"You've had quite a night. Are you sure you're, okay? I could stay a while longer." Shawn's voice was low and thick, like warm molasses. Every word flowed through her, igniting each nerve as it made its way to her lower regions.

"I'm still a little edgy. What if the truck comes back?" Janie leaned into his muscular chest, smelling the spice of his cologne and the musky smell unique to him. She tightened her grip around his neck and leaned back to look at him.

Shawn smiled as he looked down at her. It was not fear he saw in her eyes. "I think I better stay a while and make sure the truck doesn't come back."

Janie licked her lips. "If you stay, it will be for more than a little while."

Shawn grinned that special grin that meant so much more than words ever could.

Janie took his hand and led him to the

bedroom.

14

The rich aroma of Kona coffee wound its way from the kitchen to the bedroom, seducing Janie's sleeping brain. She rolled over onto her back and stretched her indolent arms over her head. She sighed, drinking in the rich decadence of the smell. She scratched her head, smiling. She felt especially good today.

"Wait. Is that bacon?" Janie sat straight up, trying to make sense of the wonderful smells teasing her nose. The pieces started to fit together—Shawn stayed here last night. This must be his doing. Either that or Mrs. Mendez is fixing a delicious breakfast again. Mrs.

Mendez lived two doors down and always flooded the complex with mouth-watering aromas. Janie hoped this time the smells were coming from her kitchen instead of Mrs. Mendez's.

She pulled on her robe as she scurried to the kitchen. There stood Shawn, wearing only a towel, frying bacon and whisking eggs. As she watched, he opened the oven, releasing the heavenly scent of homemade biscuits. Janie waited for Shawn to put the hot biscuits down before sneaking up and circling his waist with her arms. He smelled good, a mixture of soap and shaving cream.

"Mmmm," she purred into his neck.

"Well, good morning, Sunshine. I was wondering when you would get up. Do you always sleep the day away?"

Janie frowned and looked at the clock above the stove.

"Hey, it's my day off and besides, it's only eight o'clock. What time did you get up?"

"I've been up since six. I went for a run and decided to fix breakfast. Realized you didn't have any food. Went to the store and picked up a few things. Came back, took a shower, and started breakfast. Oh, I did check on you a few times. You're really cute when you're asleep."

"You did all that before eight o'clock on your day off? What's the matter with you?"

"Hey, I've got things to do. I was hoping you'd get up so we could do them together." Shawn grabbed a plate of bacon and the biscuits and sat them on the table. He dumped the eggs in a bowl. "Want to grab a couple of cups and pour us some coffee?"

Janie picked two large mugs from the cabinet. "Do you like cream or sugar?"

"No, if it's not sweet enough, I'll have you dip your finger in it."

Janie frowned at him and then smiled as she realized what he meant.

"You are such a cornball."

"A cornball? What's that?" Shawn asked.

"You know. Corny, like off the cob. Cornball," Janie explained.

Shawn just smiled at her. He reached into the fridge and pulled out the orange juice.

"Is that fresh squeezed orange juice?" Janie exclaimed.

"If you call orange juice from a box freshly squeezed, then—Yes. Yes, it is freshly squeezed."

"You're making fun of me."

"No, I just think you're the cornball. A cute cornball. But definitely a cornball."

Janie took the glasses of juice and sat them on the table. Then she punched Shawn in the arm.

"Ouch. That hurt." Shawn rubbed his arm, but the smile on his face gave him away.

They both sat down and began filling their plates. Janie took a bite of the eggs. "This is good!" she exclaimed. "Where did you learn to cook?"

"I'm glad you like it. My mom taught me to cook when I was a kid. She always said, 'no son of hers was going to leave home without knowing how to cook, do laundry and iron his own shirt.'"

"I like your mom," Janie said as she bit into a biscuit with butter dripping off it. "Mmmmm." She licked her lips and took another bite. "You said you had things to do today. What do you have planned?"

Shawn took a sip of his coffee. "I wanted to stain that table we got at the flea market, then start on your rocking chair. Have you had a chance to work on your dresser?"

"First, let's make it clear—it's not my rocking chair. I don't care if I ever see it again. Secondly, I've sanded and painted my dresser. Now I'm ready to add the poster."

"I still don't know what a poster has to do with a chest of drawers, but I'm looking forward to finding out. I'm going out to my parent's house to work on my stuff. Do you think your dresser would fit into my trunk?"

"Not without scratching the paint. It's okay, I'd rather just watch you."

"Are you sure?"

Janie took another sip of coffee. "Sure, sounds like fun." She popped the last bite of biscuit into her mouth as Shawn picked up her plate.

"I'll do the dishes while you take a shower. You have ten minutes or I'm leaving without you."

Janie stood and saluted. "Yes, Sir."

"Make that nine minutes."

She hurried to the bedroom and found a pair of jeans, a tee shirt, and underwear. She heard a ringing sound and realized Shawn had left his phone in the bedroom. Steeling a glimpse of the caller ID, she recognized the name of the caller. Charley.

"Shawn, your phone is ringing. Do you want me to answer it for you?"

"No," Shawn called back. "Let it go to voice mail. I'll call them back."

Janie stepped into the bathroom and turned on the shower. She heard Shawn come down the hall toward the bedroom. With the shower running, she cracked open the door and strained to listen.

"Hi Charley, what's up? Yeah, she's in the shower, so I have a few minutes. No, I haven't told her anything and don't you say anything either." A pause while he listened. "I told her we'd go over to Mom and Dad's and do some refinishing. Yeah, we will probably be there in about an hour. Okay, I'll talk to you soon."

Janie tiptoed back to the shower and climbed in. Shawn banged on the door.

"Janie, are you about done in there? We haven't got all day."

"I'll be out in a second. Got to rinse this shampoo out of my hair."

Janie leaned against the shower wall, letting the steamy water slide down her body. What was that about? Are they planning something against me? No. That can't be it. Shawn cares about me and Charley likes me. I'm sure I misunderstood. That's what happens when you eavesdrop. You end up assuming things based on one side of a conversation.

"Hey, do you need me to wash your back?" Shawn called from the bathroom door. "I'm pretty good at it."

"No. I'm getting out right now." Janie turned off the water and grabbed a towel. "You should have asked earlier. I'm on a strict time limit."

"You have about thirty seconds left."

"I may need a few more minutes after all," Janie called back.

Ten minutes later, she came out carrying her tennis shoes and fastening her pants. Her hair was still wet and pulled into a ponytail. Her makeup was minimal—a bit of mascara and some lipgloss.

"Ready." She said as she smiled at Shawn. "Should I bring my car? That way, you won't have to drive me all the way home later."

"What kind of guy do you think I am? My mom would slap me if I ever tried something like that."

"Such a gentleman," Janie said as Shawn opened the car door for her. Before she could get in, he leaned in, pulling her into a warm, passionate embrace. His lips were soft and moist. His kiss, hot and smoldering, melted her insides down to her toes. Janie was quite sure her toes actually curled. When he stepped back, she fell into her seat. "Mmmmm," she cooed.

Shawn grinned, "Mmmm?"

"Mmmmm," she repeated.

Shawn's parents had a lovely home. They lived on the outskirts of town on a small acreage. The grounds were beautiful, with large oak and pecan trees, several fruit trees, and hedges of boxwood at the entrance. His mother had planted flowers everywhere, giving the property the appearance of a Monet painting. Shawn led her to a large barn behind the house. Its reflection mirrored in a small pond, shining with sunlight and shaded by large tree limbs.

"It's beautiful," Janie whispered as she watched the breeze ripple across the water.

"Thanks," Shawn said. "My house is on the other side of the pond. It's not near as big as Mom and Dad's but it's mine."

He took her hand and led her to the barn. The old table sat in an area cleared of dust and straw. The walls were covered with makeshift shelves and pegboards filled with tools. A bucket of paint sat on the floor with some paintbrushes, sandpaper and old rags. A broom leaned in the corner.

He had removed the old finish from the table and sanded it smooth. It was clear of dust, leaving a handsome, naked wood, waiting for its final glory. Janie walked around the table, feeling the smoothness of its surface.

"Wow, what a difference. This wood is gorgeous."

"Just wait. The stain is going to bring out the grain. Then it will show its true beauty." Shawn lightly touched the wood. Janie saw the pride in his face and the love in his eyes for this once ugly duckling. This was obviously his passion.

He wiped the surface of the table one last time, making sure it was clean. Then he poured some stain into an empty coffee can and began to brush it on. The dark walnut stain transformed the wood. Janie pulled over a stool and watched Shawn. They didn't say much. Shawn was engulfed in his work. Janie felt like she was watching one of the old masters. He was creating a masterpiece, a genuine piece of art.

After Shawn wiped off the first coat of stain, he turned to Janie and offered his signature grin. "What do you think?"

"Oh Shawn, I'm amazed at the quality of work you do. This table is going to be a showpiece."

"How about a glass of iced tea while we wait for it to finish drying?"

"Sounds great."

The couple walked hand in hand across the yard to the house. A cloud of dust was coming toward them from the driveway. Janie watched as the dust turned into a big, black truck with tinted windows. A shiver went down her spine. Charley.

"How's it going?" Charley called, waving.

Shawn stopped and waited for her to catch up with them. He gave her a hug. Then Charley gave Janie a hug. It felt uncomfortable for Janie. She wasn't sure why. She felt resentment toward Charley and felt guilty for feeling that way. Janie decided it was the black truck and how touchy-feely Charley and Shawn seemed to be.

The threesome walked to the house. Shawn

FRIEND OR FOE

and Charley were laughing and teasing each other while Janie walked along quietly. She noticed that Shawn let go of her hand as soon as he saw Charley's truck heading that way. Now she felt like a third wheel. Wasn't this supposed to be her date? Why would Charley think it was okay to join them?

"Mom. I'm in the kitchen. Are you here?" Shawn called as they entered the back door.

"I'll be right there," called a voice.

The banter between Charley and Shawn continued as Shawn took a pitcher of iced tea from the refrigerator. Janie tried to join in and Charley and Shawn would politely include her from time to time, but they always ended up with some joke that didn't include her.

A handsome woman entered the room. She pulled her hair into a messy bun. Her eyes crinkled as she smiled at her son and the girls.

"Shawn, I wish you would have told me you were bringing guests." She patted some loose hairs into place. "I would have tried to spruce up some."

"Oh Mom, you know you don't have to make an effort for me," Charley wrapped her arms around the woman, giving her a kiss on the cheek.

"Charley, I haven't thought of you as a guest since you were five." She pulled away from the embrace and approached Janie. Taking Janie's hand, she continued. "But you are new to me. My name is Margo. Welcome to my home."

Before Janie could respond, Shawn stepped over, putting his arm proudly around her shoulder. "Mom, this is Janie. She came over to watch me work on my table."

"Very nice to meet you. You have a lovely home."

Shawn's mom smiled. Janie noticed she had Shawn's eyes. "It's nice to meet you too and thank you for the compliment on my home. We love it out here. I think Shawn does too. Have you seen his house yet? He built it himself. It's really cute."

"Mom, she doesn't want to hear about my house. We came in for tea. Why don't you join us for a minute?"

"I know you don't want to hang out with your old mom. But I will have a glass of tea with you since you invited me."

Shawn pulled out a chair for his mother and sat a glass of iced tea in front of her. Then he pulled out a chair for Janie. As Janie sat down, Charley sat a glass of tea down for Janie and another for herself. Then she took the seat beside her.

"Shawn, there are fresh cookies in the cookie jar. Put some on a plate. I'm sure you'll enjoy them."

Shawn did as he was told and brought a plate of homemade chocolate chip cookies to the table. Noticing Charley had taken the seat beside Janie, he sat in the empty chair across the table.

"Janie, Shawn tells me you work at a fabric

store. Do you sew?"

"Yes, Ma'am. My degree is in fabrics and textiles. I love anything that has to do with fabric that's creative."

"I envy you. I was never much at sewing. My seams were never straight, and I could never understand the patterns. I have started quilting, lately. I've joined a quilt club. They've been very patient in teaching me what to do."

"Quilting, now that is something I haven't done much of and I'd like to do more."

"You should come to my quilt club. I think you'd enjoy it."

"I'd love to. You'll have to give me the details."

"Come and see the table," Shawn told Charley. "That dark walnut really looks good."

"I knew it would," Charley replied. "What do you think, Janie?"

"It's beautiful," Janie answered.

"I'm the one who picked it out. I just knew that wood needed a dark, rich color," Charley continued. "I can just imagine it with a crystal vase full of pink hydrangeas in the middle of it. The vase reflecting in the glow of the table."

"Sounds lovely," Janie replied. "It was very nice meeting you," Janie offered her hand to Shawn's mother. "I'll get that information for the quilt club later. I think Shawn's ready to get back to the barn."

"He's always in a hurry to go somewhere. It was lovely meeting you, too, Janie. I hope you will come again soon."

"Okay, okay, time to go." Shawn kissed his mother on the cheek. "See you later, Mom."

Shawn led the way out of the door and toward the barn. He and Charley continued laughing and joking while Janie quietly walked beside them.

Shawn lightly sanded the table and wiped it free of dust. As he began a second coat of stain, Charley began to chat with Janie.

"So, what made you decide to come out here today?"

"Shawn invited me." Janie said flatly.

"I didn't notice your car out front. Did Shawn go pick you up?"

"Something like that," Janie responded.

"I know he worked last night, so I guess he would have picked you up this morning."

Janie said nothing. *Why is she acting like she didn't know Shawn was at my place last night? He told her I was in the shower when he called her. Is she trying to humiliate me? Well, she has another thing coming. I'm not telling her anything.*

Shawn glanced up from the table. "I went to Janie's after work last night."

Janie cringed. *What business is it of hers? I'm not a prude, but I also don't believe my sex life is anyone's business.* She crossed her arms and looked ahead to Shawn and the table.

"You mean after you left Sadie's. You joined me at Sadie's for a beer after work." Charley reminded Shawn.

Janie was shocked. *He stopped off for a beer before he came to my house. After I called and told him about the truck and the man in the parking lot. He knew I was scared.*

"You stopped for a beer before you came to my place?"

"Yeah, I told Charley I would meet her, so I did." He continued polishing the table without looking up.

"You stopped for a beer after I called you and asked for your help?"

"Yeah." Shawn stopped polishing and looked at Janie. He wasn't smiling. While Janie watched, she saw him send a look at Charley.

"He wasn't there long. Just long enough to tell me you were having trouble with that truck again," Charley explained. "It was just one beer."

"Yeah, just one beer," said Janie.

"Janie, it was no big deal," said Shawn. "The truck wasn't even there when I got there."

Janie felt the heat rising. She knew her

cheeks were getting red. In a quiet voice, she answered. "No, the truck was gone by the time you finished your one beer and got to my house. I thought you were a police officer, sworn to protect and serve. I guess that only applies to other citizens that aren't making a big deal out of nothing. After all, there was no truck when you got there. If I had known you were going to stop for a beer, I would have just called 9-1-1. But you told me to call you if I had any more problems—remember!" By the time she finished her sentence, she was no longer speaking quietly. She was hurt and humiliated. She wanted to go home, but she didn't have her car.

"Do you think you could take me home now?"

Shawn stood staring at her. "What are you so upset about?" he asked. "Just let me finish this coat and I'll take you home if you still want me to. I thought we were having a good time."

Janie felt like crying. She didn't want to wait until he was done with that coat. She didn't want to fight in front of Charley. She felt helpless. She turned and walked out of the barn.

"Wait," Charley called after her. Janie kept walking, but Charley caught up with her. "I didn't mean to cause any trouble. I'm sorry. I didn't know Shawn was coming over because you were having trouble with that truck last night. I would have told him to go right over. I thought he was talking about in general, you know, like, you were still having trouble with the truck."

"Hmmm"

"Janie, I'm really sorry. Do you want me to take you home?"

"No. Shawn is my date; he should be the one to take me home." Janie snipped.

"Yeah. He really should. What are you going to do? He's stubborn when he makes a decision. Even if he knows he's wrong."

"Don't worry about me. I'll be fine. I just need to cool down," said Janie as she continued walking.

"Well, okay. I'll let you at it then. Just don't stay out here too long." Charley stopped and watched Janie walk toward the driveway. Then she turned and went back to the barn.

Janie continued walking beyond the driveway and down the road. Pulling out her phone, she called Heather.

Ten minutes later, Heather pulled her car to the side of the road and Janie climbed inside.

"Are you okay?" Heather asked. "What are you doing way out here?"

"Long story," said Janie.

"Want to get a pizza and sit and talk for a while?"

"Sounds good."

They rode in silence until they got to Guido's Italian Inn and Pizzeria. Smells of pepperoni and cheese wafted up to greet the girls, pulling them to the buffet where they began filling their plates. They slid into a booth and signaled the server to bring two beers.

"Okay, what's going on? Start at the beginning, please."

"I'll try. I'm not sure what's going on," Janie began. She took a drink of her beer and asked the server for a glass of water. "That truck from hell was back in my parking lot last night."

"What? I hoped that was over."

"Yeah, well, it's not. This time it flashed its lights at me while I was watching from the window."

"What?"

"Yeah, only it gets worse. Shawn had told me to call him if I had any more problems, so I called him. While he was on the phone, he told me to check and see if the truck was still there. He said he was on his way. The person got out of the truck and stood in front of it. He was dressed in black and had a stocking hat over his face."

Heather stopped eating and was holding the

pizza in front of her mouth.

"Then he did one of these." Janie made a 'V' with her fingers, pointing to her eyes then to Heather's eyes, mimicking his actions.

Heather's eyes grew large. A piece of pepperoni fell off her slice of pizza.

"Shawn told me to stay away from the window. So, I did. I checked the locks and found a movie to get my mind off the parking lot."

"Let me guess—*The Birds?*"

"No, silly."

"Well, that's got to be a first. Isn't that your go-to when you're scared?"

"Ha, Ha. No, I watched *When A Stranger Calls.*" Janie took a long drink of her beer.

"What was I thinking?" replied Heather.

"Anyway, the movie was almost over by the time Shawn got there, and the truck was gone. I thought he probably had to finish some things at work before he could come by. He was saying all the right things. He made me feel safe."

"He seems like a great guy."

"Yeah, I thought so, too."

Janie went on to explain the strange phone call while she was in the shower. Charley showing up at Shawn's parent's house. Charley, letting it slip that Shawn had stopped for a beer before he came to her house.

"I just lost it. I felt like a third wheel. They were kidding around, laughing, telling private jokes. Then when I found out he had left me hanging there at my apartment while he stopped for a beer—with her, I blew up! They both acted as if I was out of line. So, I left. That's when I called you."

Heather was still for a minute. "Janie, something doesn't make sense. What is going on between these two? Do you think she still has a thing for him?"

"Yeah. I guess. I don't know. Even if she did, it would be okay if Shawn didn't play into it. I don't know what's going on, but I'm going to give them both some space. Shawn can be sweet, but I've just seen him act like the back end of a donkey."

Heather shook her head. "It's called an ass, Janie. You just saw him act like an ass."

15

Restless, Janie paced from her living room to her dining room and back again. She tried to watch a movie but could not concentrate. Her mind was on Shawn and his bizarre behavior. Last night, he was so passionate and loving. This afternoon, he behaved differently once Charley was on the scene. What about Charley?

It's obvious they have a bond. If they are a couple, then why pretend they're not? Janie sighed. I thought he was so special. Now I don't know what to think.

She replayed the morning in her head.

Shawn had been sweet, but not as passionate as the night before. Janie could explain that as being focused. *He's probably a morning person. Gets out of bed fully awake, ready to take on the day. I take longer to get moving in the morning. How else could he run first thing in the morning?*

Her mind drifted back to the night before. He was so wonderful. His desire for her was all-consuming, like a single spark igniting the kindling of her soul.

Janie wrapped her arms around herself. She had given her heart to Shawn, and she thought she had his. *What happened today? What changed?* A tear of frustration tracked down her face. *Was I wrong about last night? Was he using me?*

She decided she needed sleep. Maybe things would make sense in the morning. Janie pulled on an oversized tee shirt, brushed her teeth, washed her face, and crawled into bed. Shawn's cologne remained on her sheets. She.

breathed in his scent and knew last night was true and honest. His feelings for her were real. She rolled over and wondered if she had overreacted.

Da-da, da-da ...

Janie jumped at the sound. She picked up her phone and looked at the clock. Twelve-thirty. Who would be calling at this time of night?

"Hello," Janie whispered into the phone.

Silence.

"Hello," Janie said, louder this time.

Silence.

"What do you want?" Janie yelled.

Silence. Then the call disconnected.

"I am tired of this. Just leave me alone," she screamed at the phone.

She took deep breaths to calm herself and closed her eyes to try to sleep. She dreamed of making love with Shawn. Of a black truck watching them, flashing its lights. Charley laughing and telling Janie that Shawn was just her friend but then slipping into his arms. Shawn laughing with Charley.

Da-da, Da-da, ….

Janie jerked awake, sitting straight up.

"Hello," she yelled.

Silence.

"What do you want?"

A pause. Then, "You."

A chill ran down her spine. The mechanical voice turned her body to ice.

She disconnected the call and threw the phone to the bottom of her bed. Who is doing this? Wide awake now, Janie climbed out of bed.

She tiptoed to the living room and straight to the window. She separated the blinds with her icy fingers. There it was. The black truck. Janie stepped away from the window. Frustration and fear coursed through her. She took a few steps back, then turned and took a few more steps. She didn't know what to do. She went back to the window. The black truck seemed to give an ominous smile. Then the lights flashed.

"He's laughing at me."

Janie backed away from the window and stood staring at the closed blind.

Call 9-1-1. Having a plan of action, she headed for the bedroom to get her phone. As she went, she thought of what she would say to the operator. *A black truck has been stalking me. He's outside right now. Come quickly.* As she picked up her phone, she predicted what the operator would say. *Who's in the truck? Why do you think the truck is stalking you? Have you been threatened in any way? We can't do anything until something happens that shows the black truck is threatening harm. Call us back if something happens.*

Janie left the phone on the bed. She went back to the living room and checked the locks. She put the chain on the door and looked out the peephole. The hall outside was empty and well-lighted.

Wide-awake she went to the kitchen and

put on a pot of coffee. She grabbed her frying pan and went to the couch. Janie picked up the remote and started flipping through channels. There had to be something on to distract her for a while. She settled on *Murder She Wrote* reruns. Sipping her coffee, she watched Angela Lansbury find the clues the police missed and solve the murder.

Wonder if Angela is available for house calls?

After three episodes of the eighty's television mystery show, exhaustion took over. Janie pulled an afghan around her and fell into a deep, dreamless sleep; hugging her frying pan as if it were a teddy bear.

Suddenly Janie's eyes flew open. Adrenaline was pumping, and she was ready to run. But why? Janie lay still, listening for a sound that should not be there. Silence. She sat up slowly, quietly. She felt for her frying pan; it wasn't there. She looked under the afghan. Nothing there. On the floor, still nothing. Where is that frying pan?

The only light in the room was from the television. A late-night talk show was on. Some host she didn't recognize was doing his monologue, and the audience was laughing. She stared at the television. She didn't like talk shows. She checked her watch. Three o'five. She had slept about an hour. She picked up the remote and flipped back to the channel she had been watching. Angela Lansbury was on another adventure. So how was her channel changed to a talk show?

Janie picked up her coffee cup. Empty. She went to the kitchen for a refill, but when she lifted the pot, it was empty. She stared at the pot. She knew she made a full pot, and she only drank one cup. Who emptied the pot? As her mind tried to process the mystery of the coffeepot, she noticed another cup in the sink, half-full of coffee. Who put that cup there? She had filled the dishwasher. There were no dishes in the sink earlier. Did I put the cup in the sink? Her mind was racing.

She walked through the dark to check the locks on the door. The safety chain hung limp, not engaged. She tried the door. It opened. The door wasn't locked! Panic filled her like icy fingers going down her spine. She swallowed a scream and tried to breathe. In and out. In and out. *Make yourself calm. Panic won't help. Think!*

Shaky fingers locked the door and put on the safety chain. Her feet were heavy as she made her way back to the window. The black truck was still there. As she watched, he flashed his lights again. Janie continued to stare. She couldn't move. Her mind felt like mush, slow and sticky, unable to process the facts in front of her.

She turned back to the couch. Where is the frying pan? She dug through the cushions, looked under the couch, and checked the coffee table, all the while knowing it was gone. Was someone in my house?

The thought of someone being able to get that close to her while she slept horrified her. *I could have been killed*! She crept to the bedroom. As she stepped through the doorway, she froze. Her bed was made. The frying pan lay in the middle of the bed with her phone sitting inside. Frantically, she turned to see if anyone was behind her. She checked under the bed. In the closet. Behind the curtains.

Janie ran to the bathroom, checked behind the shower curtain, and looked in the clothes hamper. She was primal now. Searching for an unknown predator. Trying to stay alive.

Grabbing the frying pan, she went back to the kitchen for a knife. It was time to build an arsenal. She was not sure what she was up against. Whatever it was, she was going to fight.

DEBBIE ANDERSON

16

Janie planted herself on a chair near the window so she could watch the truck. She did not hide. She did not back away. She stared.

Once, the truck flashed his lights at her. This time, however, she didn't flinch. She continued to stare, daring the menacing truck to do something. Sometime around four o'clock, the truck's engine started and, with a last flash of lights to Janie, drove away. The black truck was gone. *But for how long? Why leave at four? Does the time mean anything?*

Taking a spiral notebook, Janie drew lines vertically across the horizontal lines of the page, making a chart. She labeled the left column 'date and time', the next 'activity', then, 'thoughts and conclusions', and finally, 'plan of action'. With careful precision, she logged everything that had happened over the last forty-eight hours. She put down her pen and studied the ledger, hoping for a pattern to emerge. Nothing yet.

Da-da, Da-da, …

Janie glanced at her phone. It was Shawn, again. He had called her several times during the night, but she didn't answer. She needed time. Time to determine if he genuinely cared about her or if this was all an ugly game. Janie noted the call on her log with the comment, 'didn't answer.'

She felt violated and helpless. Someone came into her house while she slept. They touched her things, used her dishes, drank her coffee, and made her bed. Whoever it was didn't break in. They came in through the door—the door she locked. They got past the safety chain—the chain she fastened. The creepiest part of all was they did it without waking her. Nothing was taken. They weren't here to rob her. They were messing with her head—making her doubt herself.

Scooping coffee into the coffeemaker, Janie began to make her plan. She wanted to feel safe and in control. Lifting her chin high, she shut the past events away for later consideration. For now, she was going to be strong.

She began humming the 70's, Helen Reddy song, *I Am Woman*. It had been one of her mother's favorite songs. Janie would watch with fascination as her mother vacuumed, belting out the lyrics over the vroom of the motor. 'Come on Janie, sing with me'. Janie would grab the dust cloth and dance around the room, stopping briefly from time to time to brush the rag lightly over the furniture. By the time the carpet was clean, they were nearly shouting the words to the chorus.

Janie filled her cup with fresh coffee and popped a bagel into the toaster. For a moment, she pictured Shawn standing in a towel, cooking bacon. Damn, he is sexy.

He called several times during the night, but Janie didn't answer, nor had she listened to any of his messages. She wanted her mind clear and focused on the situation. She couldn't risk the influence of his words or body.

Forcing the thought from her mind, she grabbed the toasted bagel and smeared it with cream cheese. She set the table, placed the bagel on her prettiest dish, and poured orange juice into a stemmed wine glass. This was probably only the third time she had eaten at the table. She liked it, she decided. She deserved it. No more waiting for special occasions, she thought. I am special enough and I deserve to be treated this way.

When she finished breakfast, she dabbed her mouth with a napkin and sighed with satisfaction. Her new resolve took over. She would no longer be a victim. She was now in charge.

She stepped out the door, locking it behind her.

First stop, the police station. It was time they were aware of the black truck and how it was stalking her. She also wanted it on record that someone had been in her house.

***

The police station was a non-descripr building on a busy intersection a few blocks from Janie's apartment. A large American flag flapped in the wind from a tall flagpole standing vigil over the front of the government building. Janie stepped up to a large, scarred desk and informed a uniformed officer she needed to file a report. A few minutes later, a bear of a man called her name.

"Officer McNamara," said the man, offering her a large hand. "Follow me, please."

He pointed to a gray metal chair beside a gray metal desk, in a sea of other gray desks.

"Coffee?"

"Yes, please." Janie answered.

Officer McNamara stepped over to a tall file cabinet with a coffeepot sitting on top. He poured coffee into two Styrofoam cups, picked up a sugar packet and the creamer container, and held them up for Janie. She shook her head and he nodded. Then he doctored his own cup with seven packets of sugar and a long pour of powdered creamer. Janie grimaced as she watched him prepare his coffee. Her stomach began to turn just thinking about the nasty, sweet concoction he prepared.

He sat his coffee on his desk and handed the other cup to Janie. Taking a sip, she grimaced, her lips puckering at the syrupy, thick, bitter fluid being passed off as coffee. She realized the only way anyone could drink this stuff was with lots of sugar, cream, and anything else that would mask the acid taste. Officer McNamara's lips curled slightly at the edges.

"Okay, so you have something to report," began Officer McNamara.

"I feel kinda silly now that I'm here. I know there's not much you can do, but I wanted a record of what's been happening," said Janie.

"Just start at the beginning. I'm sure you wouldn't be here if you didn't believe it was important."

Janie took a deep breath. "Alright. A large, black truck with tinted windows is stalking me. It's been going on for several weeks now and it's getting more and more aggressive." She gulped in air.

The officer looked at her without expression. "Does this truck have a name?"

"What?"

"You said you are being stalked by a truck; does it have a name?"

Janie blushed. "I don't know. Whoever is driving the truck is the one stalking me."

"A reasonable assumption." The officer

remained expressionless. "Do you know who is driving the truck?"

"No."

"When did you first decide you were being stalked?"

Janie explained the strange actions of the truck. How it had followed her home from the burger joint the first time. The way it followed beside her in the parking lot at work and how it had been parking outside her apartment. She told him about the truck flashing its lights at her and how a person dressed in black had gotten out and stood in front of the truck making a sign that he was watching her.

Officer McNamara frowned slightly as he listened. He typed her information into a report, stopping to ask questions as he went. When he finished, he ran his hand across his crewcut hair. "Has he threatened you?"

"No."

Officer McNamara shook his head and looked directly into Janie's eyes.

"I'm sure you know there is nothing we can do until someone actually breaks the law."

Janie nodded.

"That doesn't mean this situation isn't dangerous."

Janie nodded again.

"Has anything else happened other than the truck following you?"

Janie swallowed. "Yes, sir. I've been getting phone calls. Most of the time, it's just silence on the line or someone breathing. But last night I asked what he wanted, and he said 'You.'"

The officer nodded. Janie noticed a deep creases in his forehead. Worry lines, she thought. His eyes were deep robin's egg blue. They were kind, caring. Janie felt safe with Officer McNamara.

"Did you recognize the voice?"

"No. It sounded altered. Mechanical. You know, like in the movies when the bad guy calls disguising his voice."

The officer nodded. "Anything else?"

"Ummm. I think someone was in my apartment last night."

Officer McNamara stopped typing. "You mean someone broke into your apartment?"

"Yeah, I guess. My door was locked when I went to sleep, but when I woke up, it wasn't locked anymore." Officer McNamara nodded for her to continue.

"I had made a pot of coffee and drank one cup, but the pot was empty, and another cup was in the sink."

The officer started typing again. "Anything else to indicate someone broke in?"

Janie took a deep breath and continued. "I had gone to bed, but I woke up when my phone started ringing. I couldn't get back to sleep, so I got up and made a pot of coffee. I checked the parking lot, and that truck was out there. I checked to make sure the door was locked. Then I turned on some old reruns of *Murder, She Wrote*."

"I remember that show. The lady mystery

writer who was going around solving murders. Right?"

"That's it."

"Yeah, I never liked that show. Not very realistic. I like the *Law-and-Order* shows. Not that they are realistic. Solve a murder in sixty minutes—just don't happen. Believe me. People come in here expecting their issues to be solved in sixty minutes. Just don't happen."

Janie stared at Officer McNamara. He cleared his throat and looked back at the typewriter. "Anything else?"

"As I was saying, I turned on the TV. I had my cast iron frying pan with me in case I needed it. As a weapon, you know." McNamara nodded. "I fell asleep. When I woke up, the frying pan was gone. I looked everywhere for it. Then, I noticed the doors were unlocked, and the coffee was gone. I went back to my bedroom."

"Decide to get some sleep?"

"No. I was going to get my phone. I thought

about calling the police. But when I got to my bedroom, the bed was made and the frying pan and my phone were lying in the middle of the bed."

Officer McNamara's frown returned. "Any history of sleepwalking?"

"No."

"Was the truck still outside?"

"Yes, it left around four o'clock."

"In the morning?"

"Yes."

Officer McNamara was quiet as he finished typing the report.

"Anything else?"

"Not that I can think of."

"Does anyone else have a key to your apartment?"

"My parents have one for emergencies. But they wouldn't have come over in the middle of the night to make my bed and drink my coffee."

"I agree. Although stranger things have happened. Okay, Miss Alexander. As I said earlier, there is nothing we can do until a law is broken. If they stole something last night, we could handle this as a burglary, but they took nothing other than the coffee. Right?"

"Yes."

"You did the right thing coming in. We have a report now. We can start watching for a black truck and maybe we can have an officer drive past your apartment complex a few times a night."

Janie nodded.

"Meanwhile, keep your doors locked. You might want to get your locks changed or get some kind of security system. Doesn't have to be anything fancy -just something that will make a lot of noise if someone comes in. That's usually a good deterrent."

"Okay," Janie said.

"You're right to take this seriously, Ma'am. This could be someone trying to scare you— having some fun at your expense. The fact that he may have come into your home bothers me the most. He may have wanted to see if he could do it. Now, he knows. Next time may not be so nice for you."

Janie gulped and took a sip of her nasty coffee.

"Do you have a weapon?"

"Just my frying pan and a kitchen knife. I could probably borrow a shotgun from my dad."

"I don't recommend that. Most civilians are shot by their own guns. They hesitate, and the bad guys take the gun away from them. Most people don't realize how hard it is to shoot another person. Do you have any hairspray?"

"Hairspray? I've got *Aqua-Net*. I thought about using it, but decided it was a bad idea."

"Actually, it works pretty well. Hair spray stings like crazy when you get it in your eyes. Bug spray is even better. Pick up a can and keep it with you. If they attacked you, spray it in their eyes. Then run. Make a lot of noise and call the police."

"Okay. I'll do that."

"Ms. Alexander. Don't try to be a tough guy. Whatever happens, do what you have to, and get away. Call us if you need us."

He handed her his card. "My personal number is on the back. Call me anytime, day or night."

"Thanks, Officer McNamara. I appreciate you taking me seriously."

"Call me Mac."

DEBBIE ANDERSON

17

Janie walked across the police department parking lot with a deliberate step and her head high. Empowered and determined she had filed a police report. She knew there was nothing they could do to help her resolve her plight, but now there was a report—something tangent, in writing—lying on Lieutenant McNamara's desk. She was taking her life back—no more cowering under the covers with her cast iron frying pan. She was fighting back.

"I am women," she yelled as she reached her car, pumping her fist to the sky, as a symbol of power. Realizing she wasn't the only one in the parking lot, she lowered her head, wishing for invisibility, and climbed into the driver's seat. Next stop—the electronics store.

Electronics intimidated her. She had a laptop and a cell phone—who didn't? She knew how to text, take pictures, and surf the 'net. She could build an Excel chart or draft a paper on Word. Her pictures were stored in a Cloud somewhere. Beyond that, she was clueless. She was sure, security systems involved electronics—didn't they?

"What was I thinking? I don't have a clue about security stuff." Janie sat planted in the car, staring at the façade of the huge store. The little red devil, sitting on her left shoulder whispered in her ear, *what good would security equipment do you? You wouldn't know how to use it.*

An image of flashing red lights, police officers surrounding her apartment, guns drawn, ordering her to 'come out with her hands up,' popped into her head. She'd be handcuffed, paraded in front of all her neighbors, and thrown into a squad car. To make things worse, she would be wearing her oversized pink tee shirt. Her hair uncombed. No makeup on. People would be laughing and pointing.

"But officer, I'm innocent! I didn't realize the coffee maker would set off the alarm."

Janie shook her head to get rid of the image. Grabbing the door handle, she took a deep breath. The little angel on her right shoulder whispered, *You can do this. You are taking your life back. Just let someone try to come into your apartment once you have a security system.*

She lifted her chin in the air, ready to stand up to the bad guys. Her hand pulled the door handle. A big, black truck with tinted windows pulled into the space beside her. *Maybe a Starbucks run first. You need fortification*, said the angel.

Janie backed out of the parking space and sped toward the nearest *Starbucks*.

Five minutes later, she walked to her car, head high. A *Venti, Light Caramel Frappuccino*, double shot, double caramel sauce, and extra whipped cream, in one hand. A bag with two chocolate croissants and a box of chocolate-covered espresso beans in the other. Taking a long draw on the twenty-four ounces, five hundred and ten calorie concoction of pure ecstasy, her resolve returned. It's just an electronics store. They have people who decipher megabytes, gigabytes, over-bites, and electrolytes. A simple security system should be child's play for them.

The coffee and sugar did the trick. Janie was again strong and determined—a little shaky a touch of brain fog from the excess of sugar and caffeine—but ready for action.

The black truck was no longer in the parking lot, so Janie pulled into the nearest space. She popped out of her car and marched to the front door. As she entered this extra dimension of the galaxy, she panicked. Frantically, she looked right, and then left, turned in a circle, grabbed her hair with both hands and emitted a silent scream.

Machines were humming, lights were blinking, and automated objects were speaking mechanically. She expected to see James Bond–the Pierce Brosnan version, any minute. She felt a tap on her shoulder and turned to find a short, dark-haired kid of about nineteen, complete with glasses and a pocket protector. His plastic name badge read 'Bruce.' Bruce. Really?

"Could I help you with something?" Bruce asked. He sniffed, blew his nose, and continued. "I'm Bruce. I'm here to assist you."

"Uh, yeah. Thanks Bruce. I'm in need of a security package of some kind. Or maybe just some security without a whole package," Janie stammered. "You know, just something to keep me safe. Something that makes a lot of noise to scare the bad guys away."

"Do you have bad guys?" asked Bruce. He looked around as if bad guys would be hiding around the corner.

"Yes. Not here—I don't think." Janie looked around. "Mostly at my house or following me on the street. Do you have anything for that?"

Bruce's eyes widened, and a serious demeanor enveloped him. "I know just what you need." He looked her straight in the eye. "Follow me."

Bruce led her to an aisle filled with strange looking gadgets—cameras, night-vision glasses, small grenades. Janie gulped. "Toto, we're not in Kansas anymore," she whispered to herself.

Bruce frowned at her. "No, my name is Bruce. I've never been to Kansas." He tilted his head and lifted one eyebrow. He wondered if Janie was speaking in code.

"Um, sorry Bruce. I was just talking to myself."

Bruce nodded and smiled. "I do that all the

time." Janie nodded and smiled back.

Back to the mission, Bruce pointed to a small box. "This is a good place to start," he said. "This is a doorbell with a camera in it. It syncs up to your cell phone, so if someone comes to your door and rings the bell, you can see who it is on your phone. It also has an intercom, so you can answer the door without actually opening the door."

Janie nodded. She had seen this advertised on TV. "Yeah, okay. Do you have a demo version, so I can see it work?"

Bruce directed her to a display with a door and a doorbell. Next to it, hanging on the wall, was an imitation cell phone.

"I'm going to ring the doorbell and you're going to answer using the cell phone." Bruce removed the mock cell phone from the wall; it was attached to a curly cord to make sure it wasn't stolen. He handed the phone to Janie, forcing her to stand closer to the wall. "Ready?"

"Ready," Janie replied, staring at the phone.

Bruce rang the doorbell. Janie stared at the phone. It was blank. Bruce rang the doorbell again. Janie stared at the phone. "I don't think this is working. It's just a blank screen."

Bruce looked at the phone in Janie's hand. "Did you turn it on?"

"I didn't know I was supposed to."

"How else are you going to answer the door?"

Janie looked at Bruce, walked to the display door, and opened it. Bruce glared at her. "Why'd you do that?"

"That's how I answer a door."

Bruce sniffed. Janie was sure she saw him roll his eyes behind his coke-bottle lensed glasses. "Let's try this again." He handed the phone back to Janie, showing her what icon to push when she hears the doorbell ring.

Bruce rang the bell. Janie pushed the button to answer the call and put the phone to her ear. "Hello."

This time Janie definitely saw an eye-roll.

"Okay, you almost had it," Bruce was speaking very slowly now, as if he was instructing a toddler. "Only, instead of putting the phone to your ear, you're going to just answer it and look at the screen."

Janie nodded. Bruce rang the bell. Janie pushed accept and watched the screen. There was Bruce. "I can see you," Janie exclaimed.

"Good," said Bruce. "Now say, 'who is it?'"

"It's you. I can see you."

Bruce blew his nose. "Yes, I know. Just humor me."

"Who is it?" Janie asked in a singsong voice.

"The UPS man," Bruce answered.

"You work for UPS, too?"

"No. I'm pretending to be the UPS man who has come to deliver a package."

"Oh. Okay. Let's try it again."

Bruce rang the bell. Janie accepted the call, kept her eyes on the screen, and said, "Who is it?"

"The UPS man."

"Okay, I'll be right there."

Janie started to open the display door.

"No. Just say, 'I'm busy. Leave the package by the door.'"

"Why would I say that if I'm just sitting there in my apartment?"

"What if you were in the shower?"

"I don't take the phone in the shower."

"What if you weren't home?

"Then I'd say I'm not home right now, but if you want to wait, I'll be there in ten minutes."

Bruce dropped his face into his hands. He pulled his hankie from his pocket and blew his nose again. Then, with a deep breath, he tried again. "Maybe if you understood the purpose of this device."

Bruce explained the purpose of the security doorbell in pain-staking simplicity. After several questions and a dozen more practice runs, Janie finally answered the phone, pretending to be miles away from home, and had the UPS man leave the package on the doorstep.

"So, if someone you don't know shows up at your door, you can tell them you're in the middle of something and can't come to the door. That way, you won't open the door for a bad guy."

Janie nodded. "I get it now. I need one of these. What else do you have?"

Bruce removed his glasses and wiped them on his dirty hankie. Janie noticed without his glasses he looked very much like a young Pierce Brosnan. He took a deep breath and pushed on. "How about a security alarm?"

Five hours later, Janie practically skipped to the car. She held the receipt for her new, bare-bones, security system, which just happened to be on sale, a card with the appointment time for the techs to come and set it up, a bag with a pair of virtual reality glasses, and a date with Bruce.

She started for home, humming the Secret Agent Man song and wondering what her spy name should be.

18

Janie enjoyed the ride home from the electronics store. She was making things happen, no longer a victim but an Amazonian warrior. She was Katniss Everdeen of the Hunger Games; She-Ra: Princess of Power; and Hermione Granger from Harry Potter all rolled into one.

Just one more stop before she goes home. She had to ask her apartment manager to change her locks. She'd do it herself, or at least ask her dad to do it for her, but her lease required any changes to the locks to go through the manager. 'The office personnel must be able to enter your apartment in case of an emergency.' Fair enough.

A bell on the door chimed as Janie entered the office. Mrs. Keller beamed a dazzling smile from behind her desk. "Ms. Alexander. What an unexpected pleasure. I haven't seen you in—what?—forever! Can I get you a coffee? A tea?" Mrs. Keller jumped up, teetering on six-inch heels, took Janie's hand, and led her to a break room in the back of the office. "So, tell me, what's new in your life? I want all the gossip."

Janie pulled out a metal chair from the small metal table and sat down. "Oh, not much. You know, I just finished school so I'm working at the fabric store. Giving demonstrations, refinishing furniture, watching old movies ... same 'old stuff."

"Um-hum, Um-hum. What about your love life? Pretty girl like you—bet you have them beating your door down." Mrs. Keller sat two cups of coffee on the table and took a seat.

"Nothing really. An occasional date, but no one special."

"What about that cute cop you've been seeing?"

Janie spewed coffee all over the table and Mrs. Keller's pretty mint green silk blouse. "I am so sorry. Here, let me get you a damp towel. I think you'll want to dab it, don't rub it." She grabbed the towel and went to work, dabbing.

Mrs. Keller grabbed Janie's hand and took the towel away. "It's okay. I'll take care of it. These things happen." Her voice was crisp and cool. Janie watched as the manager took a bottle of club soda from the refrigerator, poured some on the towel, and began dabbing at her blouse.

"I'm sorry. Please, send me the cleaning bill. I'm just surprised. How did you know I was dating a cop?"

Mrs. Keller took a final swipe at her blouse and dropped the towel on the table. Gossip was always more fun than worrying over the ruined fabric. "Well, he came in here. He wanted to know some background information about you."

"What? What kind of information?"

"Oh, you know. Where you were from. If you have family close by. What you did. If you were dating. You know the usual."

Appalled, Janie glared at the manager. "That's very personal information. Why did he need it?"

"I don't know. You know me, I'm not nosy. Not my business." She made a gesture of locking her lips and throwing away the key.

"So, what did you tell him?"

"I answered his questions. At least some of them. I didn't know all the answers or his reasons for asking them. Then when I told him I didn't think you were dating anyone, he smiled and said *he* was dating you."

"He's so cute," Mrs. Keller continued. "I'm so happy for you. You two make a wonderful couple. Tell me—how'd you meet?" She propped her elbows on the table, rested her head in her hands, and smiled at Janie, waiting for the whole story.

"I accidentally hit him with a bagel," Janie answered.

Mrs. Keller threw her hands in the air as if this were the best story ever. She tossed her head back and laughed. "Oh my. Tell me more."

"That's about it."

Mrs. Keller stopped laughing. She was disappointed with Janie's uninformative response. "There must be more. Why did you hit him with a bagel? I know. You saw him and wanted to get his attention, so you threw the first thing you could find, a bagel."

"Not exactly. I didn't even know he was there. I just tossed the bagel out of the car because it was old and dried out. He just happened to be behind me, and it hit him." Janie shrugged.

"Isn't that romantic?" Mrs. Keller was smiling again, tilting her head as if she were hearing the greatest love story of all times.

If only she knew. "Mrs. Keller, I need to have the locks changed on my doors."

The dreamy face snapped to attention. "Why? You know we don't just change locks without a reason. Did you give your keys to someone not on your lease?"

"Just my parents. That's not the reason I need the locks changed. Someone came into my house last night while I was asleep."

Mrs. Keller's eyes showed alarm. "Oh my. Were you hurt? Who was it? Was it that good-looking police officer sneaking into your bed?"

"What? No. I don't know who it was. I do know they didn't break in, so they must have had a key."

"No one would have your key except you, me, and the maintenance guys. You know them—Tom, Larry, and Manuel. Therefore, the only other people with a key would be your parents. That's probably who it was. Just call your parents and tell them to bring the key back and quit coming into your apartment while you're asleep."

"Mrs. Keller ..." Janie began.

"Please call me Sandy. Mrs. Keller is too formal. Besides, Mr. Keller left years ago."

"Sandy. First, my parents didn't come into my apartment. They would have called first and even if they didn't, they would have knocked and woken me up. Second, I don't know these maintenance guys—Tom, Larry, and what was the last one?"

"Manuel. Why don't you know them? They've been here at least two months, except for Manuel; I just hired him a few weeks ago. They are all very friendly. You need to get out more, Honey."

"Which one will change my locks?"

"So, we're back to that. Personally, I do not

think you have a good reason to change your locks, but since you are such a great tenant—and friend–I'll do it. Do not make a habit of it and please do not tell your neighbors. I don't want everyone asking for new locks."

"I promise. I will tell no one. So, who is going to change them, and at what time?"

"Oh, Janie, I don't know." Mrs. Keller waved her hands dramatically above her head. "It will be Tom, Larry, or Manuel. I'll send them between eight o'clock and five o'clock tomorrow. Anything else?"

"Eight and five? Can we narrow that down to a window of an hour or two?"

"You are so demanding. The guys work from eight to five. Every morning I give them a list of jobs to do that day and they do them. The best I can tell you is it will be sometime between eight and five. So, stick around until they come, okay? If you must leave, let me know and we'll reschedule."

"If I must leave, why don't they use their key

and change the locks?"

"Why? Don't you plan to be home? You're the one that is demanding new locks. I guess I could put you down for Thursday."

"No. Tomorrow is fine. I will be home all day. Would you consider putting me at the top of their list for tomorrow?"

"Honestly. You are giving me a headache. I'll put you on the top of the list."

Janie stood up and took her cup to the sink. "Thank you, Sandy. I know this is asking for a lot. It's important to me. I want to feel safe."

"Of course you do, dear. I'm more than happy to help."

Mrs. Keller linked arms with Janie and walked her to the office door. "It was so good to see you. Come back soon so we can chat. Bring that hunky police boyfriend with you." Mrs. Keller winked.

"I'm not dating the hunky cop."

"Whatever you say, dear." Mrs. Keller winked again.

The bell on the door chimed as Janie left the office. She felt exhausted. It was time to go home and lock the door behind her.

19

Janie inserted the key into her door lock, realizing this would be the last time she would do so with this key. She was feeling empowered. Tomorrow, she would have a new lock and a security system. She was taking charge of her life.

Something seemed off as she stepped into her apartment. She looked around the living room. It looked the same. But did I leave the blinds open? She tried to remember if she opened the blinds before she left. She didn't think she had. Stepping to the window, she glanced out onto the parking lot. At least there's no black truck.

She turned and walked to the dining room. A huge arrangement of flowers sat in the middle of her dining room table. Her heart raced. She picked the card from the bouquet. 'I'm sorry. Please forgive me,' it read. No signature.

Janie dropped the card and took a few steps back from the flowers. I suppose they could be from Shawn. She looked for the name of the florist, but the card and envelope were blank other than the message.

I guess Mrs. Keller could have accepted them for me. She wouldn't dream of telling me they were here. It would ruin the surprise. She's probably spying on me somewhere outside, waiting for my response.

The smell of barbecued meat coming from outside assaulted Janie's nose. The aroma made her stomach growl. She realized she hadn't eaten since her breakfast bagel. Time to fix dinner. She would ask Mrs. Keller about the flowers tomorrow.

Opening the refrigerator, she discovered potato salad, fruit skewers, and Jell-O fluff salad. She slammed the door. Slowly, she pulled the door open again. *I did not put this food in here.*

She considered Mrs. Keller filling her fridge and decided it wasn't Mrs. Keller's style. Mrs. Keller is a snoop, not the refrigerator fairy.

As she tried to think of a reasonable explanation, the patio door opened, and Shawn walked in carrying a platter of steaks straight from the grill. Janie blinked in surprise.

"What are you doing here?" she asked.

"You wouldn't return my calls, so I decided to come by and fix you dinner."

"You what? Why would you do that?"

"I wanted to see you. You left without saying goodbye the other day. I was worried about you. I kept trying to call you, but you wouldn't answer. I decided, either something happened to you, or you must be mad at me so I decided to come by and make sure you were okay. Then I decided to make you a steak dinner. I'm rather good with the grill." Shawn grinned and held up the platter of meat.

Janie was stunned. "I don't get it. If I wasn't answering your calls, why would you think I'd want to see you?"

Shawn looked as if she slapped him. "Are you saying you don't want to see me? You don't even want to talk about whatever I did to make you mad?"

Janie glared at him, then looked at the steaks. Her stomach rumbled, reminding her she was hungry. It wouldn't hurt to hear him out. They could talk over dinner.

"Okay. We should talk about it. I had planned to take some time, so we could both think about things, but you've gone to a lot of trouble. I guess it will be okay to talk about it over dinner."

Shawn grinned again and sat the steaks on the table. "That's what I thought."

He made his way to the refrigerator and started handing the side dishes to Janie. Once everything was on the table, he pulled out her chair and waited for her to take a seat.

"Thanks," said Janie as she sat down.

Shawn took his seat. He lifted a large steak and placed it on Janie's plate, then took one for himself. "Help yourself," he said, motioning to the rest of the food on the table.

Janie took a spoonful of potato salad and passed the bowl to Shawn.

"How'd you get in?" she asked as she helped herself to a fruit kabob. "Did Mrs. Keller let you in?"

"That Mrs. Keller is a sweetheart, isn't she?" Shawn took a bite of his steak. He poured some steak sauce on his plate and dipped another bite into it.

"So, Mrs. Keller let you in?"

"No. I didn't say that," said Shawn, between

bites.

"Then how did you get in?"

"With my key," Shawn replied, as if it were an obvious answer to a ridiculous question.

"Your key? How did you get a key to my apartment?" Janie demanded.

Shawn took a large bite of potato salad and popped it into his mouth. Then he put up his finger. A sign that his mouth was full, and she should wait a second. Janie watched. She wasn't smiling.

Shawn swallowed and took a sip of his wine. "Remember the other night when I stayed over, and we made love…?"

"Of course, I remember. What does that have to do with you having my key?" Janie placed her fork on her plate and scooted her chair away from the table. She couldn't eat and discuss this situation. She wanted answers.

"Well," said Shawn, sheepishly, "The next morning, when I went to the grocery store …" He looked at Janie and raised his eyebrows, wanting a sign that she remembered this.

Janie nodded. "Go on."

"I didn't want to wake you when I got back, so I found your key sitting by your purse and took it with me. While I was out, I had a copy made. That's how I have a key. Oh, and I put your key back where I found it." Shawn acted as if this explained everything. As though it was the natural thing to do.

Janie glared at him. "Unbelievable. So, you just took my key and had one made for yourself without even asking me?" She was trying to keep her voice calm, but she was fuming inside.

"Well, yeah. I mean, we had just slept together. We had a beautiful night of passionate lovemaking. I assumed you wouldn't mind," Shawn responded, his hands out in front of him as if he were holding the situation up to show her.

"Well, I do mind." Janie stood up, her face turning red, her voice growing louder. "Just because we slept together does not give you the right to help yourself to my key. It doesn't mean you can come into my apartment whenever you like. It doesn't mean…" Janie stopped mid-sentence. She looked at Shawn incredulously. "Did you come into my apartment last night while I was asleep?"

Shawn lowered his eyes like a child caught raiding the cookie jar. "Yeah, I did. But wait," Shawn looked at Janie with pleading, puppy dog eyes, "I only came in because I couldn't reach you on the phone. I was afraid something might have happened to you. You just left. You didn't say goodbye. You didn't have a car, so you were walking home. I know how dangerous that can be. I am a police officer, you know. I was worried."

Shawn stood up and reached for Janie's hands. "I'm still not sure why you left. You scared me. Charley said you must be mad at me."

"Charley said." Janie exploded, "Charley

said." Janie pulled her hands away from Shawn and crossed them at her waist. "Well, if Charley said it must be true." Janie lost all her composure at the mention of Charley.

Shawn stood with a puzzled expression on his face. "Don't you like Charley? I thought you two were getting along. I know Charley likes you."

"Well, that makes everything okay, doesn't it?" Janie shouted, "As long as Charley's happy, then why should I be upset?"

"Wa... wa...umm," Shawn's mouth opened and closed, reminding Janie of a fish.

"I don't know what I think of Charley," Janie continued. "I do know she does not belong in our relationship, whatever that may be. I'm not interested in a threesome."

"A threesome?" Shawn looked puzzled. "Where did that come from? I thought we had an amazing night together. Just you and me. Where did you get the idea of Charley being involved in our relationship?"

"From you!" Janie shouted in frustration. "Every time we're together, Charley shows up. She is obviously obsessed with you, and you are obsessed with her."

Tears formed in Janie's eyes as she continued, "Shawn, I thought you were special. The other night was amazing. But when Charley showed up at your mother's house, you seemed more into her than me.

"And don't forget that you went to meet her for a drink before coming to my house after I called you for help. I think you had better decide. I don't know what your game is, but if we are going to be together, it is you and me. No one else. At this point, I'm not sure how I feel about the whole situation. I need time to think. That's why I wasn't answering your calls."

Shawn's face grew dark. He spoke with slow, deliberate words. "There is nothing between Charley and me. I've told you that. We grew up together. I have never cared for jealously in a relationship. It just tears everything apart. So, if you need time to think, I'll give you time. I thought you were special, but now I'm seeing a spoiled, jealous child. I hope you can think things through and realize I'm a pretty good catch. Then, maybe, we can go out again."

He reached into his pocket and pulled out his key ring. He removed Janie's key and slapped it on the table. Then he marched past Janie to the door.

"Shawn, wait," Janie called to him.

"Not now," he called over his shoulder. Then he slammed the door.

Janie picked up the key. A small, painted, red heart graced the large end.

She plopped into a chair; tears making tracks down her cheeks. A lump filled her throat. "What have I done?" she sobbed.

20

Morning broke with a bright sky scattered with feathery clouds. Birds sang their choruses as they searched for seeds, worms, and other bird delicacies. Janie woke with a headache.

She hadn't slept well. Tossing and turning, remembering the pain in Shawn's words the night before. Janie replayed their conversation repeatedly in her mind. She knew she was right. There were too many issues to be sorted out before she could even consider being in a relationship with him. So why did it hurt so badly?

The alarm went off, accosting the room with a loud clang that kept getting louder. Janie rolled over and slapped at the clock. It took several slaps before she finally made it stop. It was seven o'clock. Janie groaned. The maintenance guys could be here by eight o'clock to change the locks on her door.

She climbed out of bed and stumbled to the kitchen to start the coffee, then headed for the shower. By seven thirty, she had bathed and dressed. She clipped her hair on top of her head. Her teeth brushed. A coat of mascara on her blonde lashes. She headed back to the kitchen for a much-needed cup of coffee.

Once she filled her cup, she dropped a bagel into the toaster. She grabbed the tub of spreadable cream cheese and waited for the bagel to finish toasting. She pulled the hot, crusty bread from the toaster, burning her fingers as she did. A smear of cream cheese and breakfast was ready. She took her plate and her coffee cup to the table.

The coffee was hot, strong, and delicious. She held the warm cup in both hands and breathed in the nutty aroma. Then she took a sip. The hot beverage slowly made its way from her mouth to her throat, finally reaching her stomach. It was wonderful. She felt as if the coffee was making its way through her body, waking up each area as it went. She took the time to enjoy the sensation and savor every drop.

A knock on the door disrupted her ritual. Time to start the day. She found all three maintenance guys, Tom, Larry, and Manuel, standing outside her door.

"Well, if it isn't Larry, Curly, and Moe," Janie exclaimed, as she motioned for them to come in.

"No, it's Tom, Larry, and Manual," replied the three in unison.

"We're here to change your locks," Manuel explained.

"Who are Curly and Moe?" asked Larry.

"Never mind," said Janie. "Just a little joke."

The three men chuckled weakly. Obviously, they had never heard of the *Three Stooges*.

"So, it takes all three of you to change the locks?"

"Not really. It only takes one. The other two will just watch," explained Tom.

Janie nodded. "I do have two doors. The front one and the patio door. One of you could change the front door and someone else could change the patio door. Then only one of you would have to watch."

The men nodded, as if considering this novel idea.

"We don't mind watching," Manuel assured her.

Larry took a screwdriver from his tool kit and began removing the locks. Tom and Manuel plopped down on the sofa.

"Any more of that coffee?" asked Tom.

FRIEND OR FOE

"Help yourself," said Janie, pointing at the table. Before long, both men had a cup of coffee and were spreading cream cheese on their bagels.

"Too bad you don't have any eggs," Manuel stated.

"And bacon," said Tom. "I love bacon."

Janie's headache was getting worse.

"Larry, can I get you a cup of coffee?" Janie asked.

"Not right now. When I finish this door, it will be time for a break. I'll have a cup then."

Janie nodded. Tom and Manuel had taken seats at her dining room table. She took a seat on the couch.

"Hey. Where'd you get these flowers?" asked Tom between bites of his bagel.

"A friend gave them to me," Janie answered.

"They're pretty. Must be from a good friend. Maybe a boyfriend." Said Manuel, grinning at her as if he discovered a great secret.

"No. Just a friend," said Janie. She picked up a magazine and pretended to read it. As she sat there, Janie had a strange feeling, as if someone was watching her. She looked up and caught Manuel glaring at her. "Did you need something?" She asked him.

"No, I'm just sitting here," said Manuel. He continued to stare. His toothy grin made her uncomfortable. His obvious glare made her skin crawl.

"How's it going, Larry?" she asked.

"Just fine."

"Are you sure you don't need help from your colleagues?" Janie asked.

"What's a colleague?" asked Larry. "Does that have something to do with colleges? 'Cuz, I didn't go to college. I got my GED, though."

"That's good," said Janie as she dropped two capsules from her Extra Strength Excedrin bottle into her hand and downed them with the rest of her coffee.

Tom threw a piece of bagel at Manuel to get

his attention. Manuel continued to stare. Tom threw another piece. This one hit the wall and stuck there thanks to the cream cheese. Manuel continued to glare.

"Stop it," yelled Janie. "Isn't there something you can do? Maybe start changing the locks on the patio door?"

Tom looked down at his hands like a small, scolded boy. Manuel continued to glare.

"Really," Janie continued. "If one of you changes the locks on the patio door, you will finish in half the time. Then you can move on to the next thing on your list."

"We don't know how to change a lock," said Tom. Manuel smiled a sly smile as he glared some more.

"Then why are you here?" Janie asked.

"'Cuz, you needed your locks changed," Tom explained. He shook his head as if Janie were asking stupid questions.

Janie shook her head in disbelief. Tom frowned, confused, and shook his head.

Manuel grinned and kept glaring.

"Break time!" Larry declared and headed for the coffeepot.

Two hours later, both locks were changed, and Larry handed her a key. "Here ya go. Mrs. Keller said to remind you not to give a key to anyone else. I'll give her this extra one, so we can get in when we need to."

"Okay, fine," Janie answered, practically pushing them out the door. "Thanks for your help."

As she shut the door, she overheard Tom ask, "What, no tip?"

"She's pretty. I could go for some of that," said Manuel.

Janie felt like taking another shower.

Instead, she called Heather. "Hey, girl. What are you up to?"

"Nothing much. I haven't heard from you in a while. How's your love life?" answered Heather.

Janie told her about the past few days.

"Then last night, I get home and there's this gigantic bouquet on my kitchen table."

"Really? Who were they from?"

"Shawn!" Janie exclaimed.

"Well, that was nice."

"Yeah, but he broke in and put them on the table."

"What? How'd he break in?"

"With the key he made. Can you believe that? But wait, there's more. He walked in my patio door with steaks he had grilled on my grill."

"What?"

"I know, right? My refrigerator was full of potato salad and Jell-O-fluff salad, and stuff."

"I love *Jell-O* fluff salad," exclaimed Heather.

"I know, but that's not the point. The point is, he made a key without my permission and let himself into my house with all this food."

Heather thought for a moment. "Okay. I understand he shouldn't have made a key and just barged in like that. But he must really like you if he went to all that trouble and brought you flowers and steaks and *Jell-O* fluff salad."

Janie rolled her eyes. "Well, anyway, I had my locks changed. This afternoon I'm getting my security system installed. Feel like coming over? I'll put in a movie, and we can eat *Jell-O* fluff salad."

"Sounds good. I'll see you in a little while," said Heather, as visions of *Jell-O* fluff danced in her head.

A few minutes later, Bruce arrived with another technician to install the security system.

"I decided to come along so I could explain how everything works," Bruce clarified as he helped Alex, the tech, unwrap an assortment of gadgets, switches, and wires.

"Good idea," Janie mumbled under her breath.

"I'll let him set it up, then I'll explain it," said Bruce.

Janie plopped on the couch, totally perplexed by what she saw.

"Are you sure I bought all this stuff?" she asked.

"Yeah. It probably looks different because you didn't see it when it wasn't put together."

Janie nodded.

Suddenly, there was a knock at the door. Janie looked at Bruce and Alex.

"Answer it. We haven't hooked anything up yet," said Bruce.

Janie opened the door. It was Heather. "Come on in. That didn't take long."

"I'd climb a mountain for *Jell-O* Fluff salad."

"Good to know," answered Janie.

"What's all this?" asked Heather, pointing to all the gadgets and wires.

"They're installing my security system, remember?"

"I don't remember much after you mentioned *Jell-O* Fluff salad."

"I believe that. Well, this guy is Alex. He's

the technician that is installing my system." Alex blushed and smiled, then offered a sweaty hand to Heather. "And this is Bruce. He's the guy who sold all this to me. He's going to explain how it all works once it's installed."

Bruce stood and took off his glasses. He sniffed and extended his hand. "Very nice to meet you. You're beautiful." As soon as the words left his mouth, he turned crimson and clapped a hand over his mouth. "Uh, sorry. Sometimes I just blurt things out."

Heather grinned. "That's okay. It was nice." Bruce and Heather sat down, side by side, and stared at each other. Janie shook her head.

"So, do you still want *Jell-O* Fluff?"

Heather continued to stare at Bruce and he at her. "Yeah. I still want *Jell-O* Fluff Salad."

"I love *Jell-O* Fluff Salad," said Bruce.

"I'd take some *Jell-O* Fluff Salad, if it's okay," chimed in Alex.

"Sure. Let's take a break and eat *Jell-O* Fluff salad."

21

It had been a strange day and Janie was tired. She had new locks on her doors and a new alarm system, which Bruce had explained to her several times. She spent all afternoon with her friends setting up the alarm system, watching movies, and eating *Jell-O* Fluff Salad.

Heather and Bruce fell instantly in love, or at least, infatuation. When they left a few minutes ago, they still had hearts floating over their heads. Guess her date with Bruce was canceled on a technicality—called Heather. Janie was happy for them and glad to see

Heather back in the saddle, so to speak.

Janie checked the alarm system. It was set and ready with the appropriate lights glowing, assuring her it was on the job. "Just try to get in now," she dared whoever might want to try. She turned off the lights and went to bed.

Feeling relaxed and safe, it didn't take long before she was sound asleep. Soon she was dreaming. Heather and Bruce were a single entity, floating around with connecting hands and feeding each other *Jell-O* Fluff Salad. Janie watched as lights blinked, and buzzers buzzed, and Brad Pitt kept telling her he wanted to take her away to a far-off land and be her sex slave. Janie smiled in her sleep as she drifted away with Brad. Then the buzzers got louder, and Brad was saying in a robotic voice, "Danger, danger, Will Robinson."

Her sleepy smile turned to a frown. "It's too loud, Brad," she said sleepily.

"Roll over on your stomach," said Brad.

Janie did as she was told. Brad grabbed her

hands and pulled them behind her. Her smile returned. "Oh Brad," she whispered, "I didn't know you were into the kinky stuff."

Brad was being too rough. He was tying her hands with a scarf—no, something else, something stronger. Her sleeping brain tried to wake up. The buzzing was getting louder. She couldn't move her arms. Now Brad was tying her legs. "Stop, Brad, that hurts," she called out.

Her conscious self was making its way to the surface. Janie tried to roll over onto her back, but a large hand held her head down into the pillow. Struggling for air, Janie woke, her eyes wide open as she realized she wasn't dreaming.

"Stop struggling and lay still," ordered a deep, masculine voice. "Do as I say, and you won't get hurt. I'm going to take my hand off your head, but do not look at me. Do you understand?"

Janie nodded into the pillow. The hand

moved from her head, allowing her to get a breath. As she gulped in air, she started to turn to find out why Brad was doing this. The hand slapped hard across her ear and cheek.

"I said don't look at me," the voice yelled.

"You're not Brad," Janie stated. She wished she could get her hands free, so she could touch her sore cheek. "That hurt. Brad would never hurt me."

"Who the heck is Brad?" asked the voice. "Just shut up and listen to me."

Janie was scared. Her brain was still fuzzy from sleep. She could hear the alarm going off. Her phone started ringing. She was getting mixed messages from her subconscious. Panic. Just lay still, Police are on their way. Panic. Panic. PANIC!

The hand was now binding her face. Around her head, covering her mouth, around her head again, covering her eyes, around her head again. Duct tape!

"We are going for a ride," said the voice. He

yanked the pillow out from under her and pulled something over her head. More duct tape tightened around her neck. She was abruptly lifted and thrown over a hard, powerful shoulder.

"Don't even try to escape," said the voice as she bounced against his muscular back.

Where are the police? How long has it been?

The person was running now. Janie felt the coolness of the night against her bare skin.

Sirens! I can hear sirens!

Janie felt herself being tossed onto something hard. She kicked with her bound feet. A door slammed, and an engine came to life. *A car*, she thought, *or a truck. THE BLACK TRUCK! Oh, no! Oh, no! OH, NO!*

Janie kicked, hoping to hit the man, or the steering wheel, or anything that could cause a delay. *I've got to stall. The police are on their way.* She could still hear sirens. She kicked harder. This time, she connected with something. The driver's leg.

"Stop that!" said the voice.

A fist slammed into her covered face. Janie tasted blood. The fist came down again. Everything went black.

Janie moaned as she regained consciousness. Everything was black, and she couldn't move. Her face hurt. *Where am I?* Hard rock music blasted. Someone was singing along, or at least trying to. The vibration of the vehicle combined with the rhythmic thump, thump, of the music was giving her a headache. She fought nausea as she tried to understand where she was.

Panic was taking control. She tried to scream, but she couldn't open her mouth. *What is happening?* Her nightmare bubbled to the top of her mind. She remembered the alarm going off and Brad Pitt yelling at her. But it couldn't be Brad Pitt, could it? Her body slid, and she was unable to stop it. Oooff! She hit something.

Sirens, she remembered sirens. *Was that real or did I dream it?* She couldn't be sure. She strained to listen. No sirens now. She remembered Bruce telling her the police were automatically called when the alarm went off. *Where are the police?*

This can't be real. I'm having a horrible nightmare. Wake up! Janie screamed to herself. *You've got to wake up!* But Janie knew she wasn't dreaming. Her face hurt. She couldn't move her arms or legs. She was rolling around in what seemed to be the floorboard of a truck. Kidnapped. Her mind became alert to her reality. He kidnapped her!. Fear raged in her whole body, causing her to shake uncontrollably.

You've got to take control. Stay calm and find a way to save yourself! Janie made herself breathe. In and out. In and out. Trying to stay calm. She realized her captor didn't know she was awake. This was good. She needed time to think.

Her thoughts jumbled. What's real and what is a dream? Her mind racing, trying to piece it together. The music thumped against the inside of her skull. She wanted to scream, to tell the monster to shut up. But she couldn't.

Stay calm, think this through.

Janie knew if whoever this was thought she was unconscious, she had some time. She had to come up with a plan.

Evaluate your assets.

Janie tried to move her arms—not happening, tied too tight.

She tried her legs. *Ankles also tied tight. Able to bend my knees.*

Unable to open my eyes or mouth.

Not much to work with.

Terror filled her. Tears rolled down her swollen cheek. Breathe. In and out.

The vehicle stopped abruptly, slamming her into the front of the floorboard. Ouch! She bit her lip to keep herself from screaming out.

When the truck started moving again, she rolled backwards into what felt like a seat. Something sharp poked her in the back. What was that? She tried to feel with her hands but couldn't find anything with her limited reach. The vehicle slowed slightly and made a turn, sending Janie rolling forward again. Okay, I think we turned right. The truck accelerated. She rolled back and was again poked by something sharp.

The driver continued singing, belting out terrifying lyrics. Janie felt like the music was inside her head, pounding against the inside of her skull. Thump, thump, thump. Her head throbbed. Janie knew as long as the music continued, her captor wouldn't be able to hear her.

Try to find a weapon. She tried to scoot back toward the seat. It was hard to do with her hands and feet bound, but it maybe her only chance. Whatever was poking her could be a tool or a knife. The thought of a knife being used on her sent chills down her spine. She had to get it before he could use it against her.

Each time the vehicle rolled her back, she tried to use her toes and knees to keep from moving forward again. It was a slow process, but eventually, she felt the sharp item that had been poking her. She carefully examined it with her fingers. It was a long, thin, metal, curly thing with a pointy end. A spring! She tried to pull it from under the seat, but it was attached at the other end. So much for a weapon.

The vehicle bumped over what Janie thought to be a railroad track, causing the spring to jab her again. *Ouch. Wait. Use it to tear the tape. Need to get my hands loose.* She began rubbing the tape on her wrists against the point of the spring. It was arduous work. She could move her arms at the elbow, pulling her bound hands up and down against the sharp spring. She scraped her hands and wrists as much as she did the tape. Her arms ached from the strain of trying to maneuver unnaturally. Her muscles tense. Blood and sweat made her wrists sticky and slick.

The vehicle stopped again, forcing her to crash hard against the seat and the spring. Janie felt the spring pop through the tape. She could feel the spring between her hands. She tried to pull her hands apart, but they wouldn't budge. She tried to pull her hands off the spring. No luck. Now she was caught on the spring. Janie did a mental eyeroll. Now what?

The crunch of tires over gravel brought Janie's attention away from the spring. The truck moved slowly. Then it stopped, and the engine turned off. The pounding music stopped, but Janie's head still kept the beat. She lay still, hoping her captor couldn't hear her heart pounding. Fresh panic sent adrenaline pumping to all her sore, achy muscles. She heard the door open. The driver's seat squeaked as he climbed out. Janie tried again to loosen herself from the spring. She could hear his footsteps walking to her door. Just as he pulled open the door, the tape tore from the spring, freeing her hands.

"Okay, pretty girl," said the man, scooping her up and throwing her over his shoulder again. "Time to meet the boss." Janie lay against his back, still holding her hands together while she tried to think of a plan. She felt him shift his weight from one leg to the next as he opened a door. This was her chance. Bringing her arms up to his shoulders, she pushed away from him, causing him to lose his hold on her. She fell off his shoulder and slammed to the ground, landing on her butt. She struggled to stand up, but with her ankles tied and a bag on her head, she couldn't get her balance.

The man laughed, reached down, and grabbed her. Janie beat on his chest, tried to find his eyes, anything that she could get her hands on. She scratched his face and pulled his hair. The man held on tighter.

He walked into a room as she struggled.

Then dropped her hard onto the concrete floor, knocking the air from her lungs. Janie gasped for a breath. Her nostrils trying to capture enough oxygen to help her breathe. As she rolled on the floor, she could feel herself growing faint.

As she lost consciousness, she heard the man say, "Here she is, boss. She's a wildcat!"

DEBBIE ANDERSON

22

Regaining consciousness, Janie tried desperately to inhale oxygen through her nose. Duct tape still covered her mouth and eyes. She needed to get the bag off her head and the tape off her mouth so she could take a deep breath. Panic seeped into every pore.

She knew she needed to calm herself so she could evaluate her options and free herself from her bondage. Her mind and body were not working together. Her mind said, Calm down. Her body said, get this thing off me so I can breathe.

Frantically, she clawed at the tape around her neck. She found the ragged edge and ripped it loose, pulling the bag from her head along with the tape. Then she started on the tape covering her mouth. As her fingers worked on the outside, her tongue worked on the inside. She moved her jaw from one side to the other and made chewing motions to loosen the tape. The stickiness began to give way. Janie grabbed the tape and jerked it from her mouth. She gulped air in loud, deep gasps. As she sucked in the delicious oxygen, she realized there were other people in the room with her.

She forced herself to stop moving and listen. She could hear voices. Angry voices. A man and a woman, arguing. They didn't seem to be paying attention to her as they fought with each other.

Janie took advantage of her opportunity and continued to work on the tape, wrapped around her head and over her eyes. Her fingers forensically explored the duct tape, moving inch by inch across the strip until she found an edge. Cautiously, she pulled, disengaging it. It pulled at her hair, sending pain through her scalp. It ripped skin and tiny hairs from her face, stinging and leaving red, raw lines. Damn, whoever did this. Tears streamed from her eyes as she worked. She fought to keep quiet, not to cry out, not to scream. As she worked, she tried to concentrate on the conversation on the other side of the room.

"Why did you bring her here? What are we supposed to do with her?" It was a female voice.

"I didn't know what else to do. Alarms were going off. I just wanted to get out of there."

"What alarms?"

"The alarms that went off once I entered the apartment."

"She has alarms? I didn't authorize any alarm system."

Mrs. Keller? It sounds like Mrs. Keller. Janie

pulled the tape from one of her eyes, pulling her eyelashes out with it.

"How should I know what alarms? All I know is, I go in and suddenly, alarms are blaring. I just grabbed her and ran."

"You idiot! Why didn't you just leave her and go?"

Janie gritted her teeth as she pulled the tape from the other eye. She wouldn't have to pluck her eyebrows for a long while. Slowly she opened her eyes and was assaulted by bright lights.

"You told me to rob her. I knew if I came back without doing that, you'd yell at me."

Janie squinted toward the voice, trying to bring her vision into focus. *I know that voice. How do I know that voice?*

"I told you to *rob* her. Not rob *her*." Janie heard a slap as Mrs. Keller's well-endowed bottom came into view, blocking the person she was talking to.

"What do you want me to do, take her back? She hasn't seen us yet. I can wait a few hours and sneak her back into her apartment."

Manuel! It was Manuel!

Mrs. Keller considered Manuel's suggestion. Janie watched as she paced back and forth in front of Manuel, blocking his view of Janie.

"I don't know. It might work. We must make sure she doesn't see our faces." Mrs. Keller turned to look at Janie. Janie froze.

"Looks like she's still out."

"Maybe, but how did she get the bag off her head?" asked Manuel.

Mrs. Keller took a few steps closer to Janie. "Yeah, and the tape off her face?"

Manuel joined Mrs. Keller as she moved closer to Janie. Janie pretended she was still unconscious. *Play dead. Play dead.* Janie told herself, then grimaced inwardly and changed her mantra to *Play unconscious. Play unconscious.*

Mrs. Keller and Manuel bent down closer to Janie.

"Is she dead?" asked Manuel, kicking her leg lightly.

"Is she breathing?" asked Mrs. Keller, kicking Janie's leg a little harder.

Manuel pulled his leg back, preparing to send Janie over the goalpost. Her eyes popped open, her hands up in a defensive stance.

"Stop that," Janie yelled. "That hurts."

Mrs. Keller and Manuel both jumped back in surprise. Janie tried to get up. Her ankles were still bound. She wobbled first in one direction and then the other and fell back to the floor. She started scooting on her rump toward the door as fast as she could make herself move.

"Get her!" Mrs. Keller pointed and stared at Janie.

"Why? She's not going anywhere." Manuel stepped in front of her, placing his huge hand on Janie's head. As hard as she tried to scoot, she was going nowhere.

"Why, Miss Alexander, wanting to leave so soon?" purred Mrs. Keller. "The party is just starting, and you're our guest of honor."

"Look, why don't you just let me go? I'm sure it was all a terrible mistake. I can forgive and forget. We all make mistakes." Janie looked up at her captors, batting her lash-less eyes and forcing a smile.

"I don't think we can do that." Mrs. Keller looked at Manuel. "What do you think, Manny, dear?"

"No, I don't think that would be possible. She's seen our faces," replied Manuel.

"I didn't see anything," Janie explained, closing her eyes tightly. "I won't say anything. Let's forget the whole thing."

"You may believe that now, dear, but what about that cute cop boyfriend of yours?" Mrs. Keller continued, "One night the two of you are cuddled together and you remember the time Manuel accidentally abducted you." Mrs. Keller used air quotes when she said accidentally.

"I'm sure you wouldn't mean any harm. Just some friendly recollections. A little pillow talk. But yummy, Officer Shawn may not see it that way."

"He's not my boyfriend!" exclaimed Janie, rolling her eyes. "We're not even friends anymore."

"Likely story. I know if he was my boyfriend, I wouldn't let him go. He's soooo sexy." Mrs. Keller swooned and licked her lips.

"I'll be your boyfriend, baby!" cooed Manuel as he stroked Janie's hair, his hand getting caught in some leftover duct tape. "I know how to make you scream!"

"Shut up!" yelled Janie and Mrs. Keller together.

Without warning, the door flew open, slamming against the concrete wall.

"Get away from her!" yelled Heather. She ran to Janie, throwing herself in front of her friend, arms outstretched, protectively.

"Yeah!" said Bruce, still standing by the

door. He took a puff from his atomizer. "The police are on their way."

Manuel laughed. His deep, sarcastic voice, echoed through the room. "Sure, they are. Meanwhile, what are you going to do, runt?"

Bruce sniffed, wiped his nose on his sleeve, and cleared his throat. "I've got this," He announced, pulling a taser from his pocket.

Manuel laughed again. "Nice try, peewee. You've got to get close enough to zap me. We all know you don't have the guts. I would flatten your skinny ass onto the floor. What do you think, Mrs. Keller? Want a new rug?"

Bruce took two steps forward and zapped him. Manuel started jerking and shaking as an electric current ran through his body. Drool rolled down his chin. His eyes rolled back in their sockets, and he fell to the ground.

Mrs. Keller took a shaky step back.

"Great job!" said Heather, and then planted a lip-lock on Bruce.

"Hey, you guys! Could someone help me

get this tape off me, please?" asked Janie.

"Sorry." Heather ran to Janie and started tearing at the tape.

"Just a minute," said Mrs. Keller. "She's not going anywhere."

Bruce aimed the taser at her. "Step back. I'd hate to hurt an old lady."

Mrs. Keller's face twitched. Her eyebrows climbed higher on her forehead, forming a V. Smoke poured from her ears. Large, cigarette-stained teeth showed through blood-red lips.

"Who are you calling an OLD LADY?" screamed Mrs. Keller. She pulled a shiny black gun from her pocket. "Last I heard, a gun trumps a taser every time."

Janie and Heather gasped and grabbed each other as they stared at the ominous gun. Bruce sniffed again. Then he bowed slightly toward Mrs. Keller, did a round-off, kicking his leg out and knocking the gun from Mrs. Keller's hand.

"Ahh, Yaaiiii!" he yelled, then bowed again toward Mrs. Keller.

Mrs. Keller stood stunned, staring at the fallen weapon.

Heather scrambled for the gun and aimed it at Mrs. Keller.

"Sandy, I thought you were smarter than that."

All heads jerked toward the voice coming from the doorway. There stood Shawn, standing what seemed to be ten-foot tall with a gun pointed directly at Mrs. Keller. Janie thought he was wearing a white hat, but it was just a shadow.

Seconds later, Charley ran in behind Shawn, dressed in black jeans, a black tee shirt, and boots, with her gun drawn. "You got this?" she asked Shawn.

"Book 'em, Danno," answered Shawn, smiling.

Beyond the door, red and blue lights flashed.

Charley ran to help Janie get the rest of the duct tape off her ankles and carefully pulled pieces from her hair.

Heather ran to Bruce, who had fainted on the floor.

Janie stared at everyone in disbelief. "What just happened?"

Shawn handcuffed Mrs. Keller, who looked at him with twinkly eyes and a toothy smile.

"I'll go anywhere with you, you sexy hunk of man."

"Just as far as the police station, Ma'am," said Shawn as he gave her a slight push toward the door. Mrs. Keller grabbed his arm with her cuffed hands, as if he was escorting her to the prom. Her eyes blinking suggestively, her eyebrows wiggling up and down, she let him escort her to the waiting police car.

Charley handcuffed Manuel, who jerked all the way to the squad car outside.

"Oh Manuel, I think you've wet yourself,"

observed Charley. "Shawn, do you have a towel or a plastic sheet or something to put on the seat?"

Heather let go of Bruce long enough to help Janie up. "Are you okay?"

"Yeah. I guess so." Janie stared at her friends in disbelief.

"Ready to get out of here?"

Janie just nodded.

DEBBIE ANDERSON

23

Janie stepped out of the building with Heather on one side and Bruce on the other. Five squad cars, complete with flashing lights, surrounded the entrance. People were yelling orders, radios were squawking, looky-loos began gathering. Janie watched as Shawn pushed Mrs. Keller's head down and helped her into a squad car. Another officer was reading her Miranda rights. Mrs. Keller continued to stare at Shawn, blinking puppy-dog eyes and cooing her devotion to him.

Manuel was standing red-faced beside another squad car, trying to hide the wet spot on his pants. Another officer watched his every move, trying to stay professional despite the powerful smell of urine wafting from his prisoner. Charley covered the seat with a rubber sheet, then asked the officer if he had any room deodorizer in his car and stared at Manuel with disgust.

The scene was overwhelming. Janie's mind flashed through images of the last six hours. She thought she was safe with the new alarm system. How could someone come into her home, her sanctuary, and abduct her? Her head hurt. Her side hurt. Everything hurt! The kicks and blows she received from Manuel and Mrs. Keller were going to leave bruises. She was exhausted and feeling slightly nauseous.

Janie scanned the scene in disbelief. How did this happen? Where did all these people come from? Her eyes tried to take in what was in front of her as she tried to make sense of it. Then she saw it. The black truck. The demon vehicle that stalked her for the past several weeks. The nightmarish conveyance of her abduction. Hatred flashed toward this piece of evil. Mentally, she knew it wasn't rational to attribute her ordeal to an inanimate object made of steel and plastic. People were the cause of her terror. Specifically, Manuel and Mrs. Keller. Emotionally, she couldn't help but feel hate toward the large, black stalker with tinted windows.

A squad car pulled out of the parking lot, giving Janie a better view of the truck. There, parked beside the black truck, was a second black truck with tinted windows. Janie swooned. Her legs went limp, and she fell to the ground, unconscious. Heather and Bruce dropped to the ground beside her, rubbing her hands and calling her name.

"We need an ambulance," called Shawn, running to Janie's side. Gently, he checked her pupils and pulse. "She's going into shock," he told the others. "She needs to go to the hospital—now!"

He held her hand in one of his large hands, noticing how small she looked. Stroking her hair as he pleaded with her, "C'mon Babe. You're tough. You can beat this."

Charley brought a blanket and wrapped it around her. "Ambulance is on the way."

Shawn didn't take his eyes away from Janie's limp body. Heather kneeled on the other side, crying quietly. Bruce stood by sobbing loudly. Sirens echoed in the distance.

***

"Janie? Can you hear me?"

"Janie, wake up. You're scaring me."

Janie frowned as her unconscious brain tried to make sense of these voices. In her mind, a big, black truck was talking to her through his large grill of a mouth. It was a sinister being. Janie knew it would eat her if she wasn't careful. She cringed and tried to back away. *But why did it sound like Heather?* She wanted to get away from this awful creature. It would take her away again. It would hit her. Kick her. A moan escaped, but she was still trapped.

"Please, Janie. Open your eyes," a voice sobbed.

Is that Bruce? Why is he crying? Why does that truck sound like Bruce?

"Janie, sweetheart, listen to my voice. It's time to wake up now. You're safe. Open your eyes."

Shawn? The black truck began to fade away. She tried to open her eyes. Her eyelids were too heavy. The effort was too much. She wanted to sleep. She gave way to the fatigue and let herself fall back into the darkness.

***

"Ms. Alexander. Janie. This is Doctor Selby. You're in the hospital. It's important that you wake up now. Can you open your eyes?"

Janie frowned. *Dr. Selby? The hospital? Why am I in the hospital? Why can't they let me sleep?*

A bright light flashed into her eyes, first one,

then the other. Janie groaned. Something was on her arm. It was getting tighter. *He's tying me up again*! Janie fought, trying to pull away from whatever was holding her.

"No, no. Get away!" she moaned.

"That's right, Ms. Alexander. Fight me. Open your eyes and fight."

Janie jerked and tried to pull away. She tried to open her eyes. They were so heavy. Were they taped shut again?

Janie struggled to get away, shaking her head, and screaming, "No, no." but she couldn't hear herself. Her attacker wasn't listening. Frantically, she tried to make herself heard, "No, No. NO" she screamed.

Her eyes flew open. She looked around hysterically and pulled herself up to the top of the bed, her knees close to her chest. Her hands tore at the blood pressure cuff and the IV stuck in her arm.

"Whoa!" the doctor called calmly, grabbing her arms to keep her from pulling out the tubes. "You're okay now."

Heather jumped up and pulled Janie into a tight hug, tears streaming down her face. Bruce cried louder, wrapping his arms around both girls.

"Ms. Alexander, I'm Doctor Selby. Can you answer some questions for me?"

Janie looked at the doctor and nodded. "Why am I here?"

"You've been through a bit of an ordeal. You have a few bruises and contusions and you're suffering from a concussion. You need rest and quiet. I want to keep you overnight. You'll probably be able to leave in the morning."

Janie nodded. "I feel like I've been run over by a truck, a big, black one."

"I'm sure you do. You'll be sore for a few days and the bruises will be pretty ugly, but with rest I'm sure you'll be fine.". Dr. Selby patted her shoulder.

"Oh, thank goodness!" shouted Heather.

Bruce nodded and blew his nose. His tears continued to fall.

The doctor turned toward Shawn. "No questions tonight. You can talk with her tomorrow."

"No problem," said Shawn. "Tomorrow will be soon enough."

A nurse came into the room holding a hypodermic needle. "Time for everyone to leave. This young lady needs her sleep." Taking the IV tube in her hands, she dispensed the contents of the syringe. Janie melted into a deep sleep.

24

The sun was shining, birds were singing, and Janie was eating a bowl of Special K with Strawberries. The nurse informed her the doctor was letting her go home in a few hours.

The door opened, and Charley walked in. She was dressed in black jeans and a black tee shirt. Her blonde hair pulled back in a high ponytail. Her freshly scrubbed face had a healthy glow. Her smile lit up the room.

"How are you feeling?" Charley asked, as she bent down and gave Janie a hug.

"Pretty good," Janie answered. "I'm sore,

but I'll be fine. The doctor said I could go home soon."

"I'm so relieved. You've been through a lot."

"So, what exactly happened? I guess you're a police officer, too."

Charley smiled. "Yeah, I'm a detective. I'm sorry I couldn't tell you everything up front."

"So, tell me about your part in this from the beginning."

"I'm the one asking the questions," said Charley. "I'm here to get your statement."

"You first," answered Janie, pushing herself back against her pillow.

Charley laughed and pulled up a chair. "Okay, where do you want me to start?"

"The beginning would be nice." Janie fluffed the pillow to make herself comfortable. Crossing her arms, she continued. "So, was it you that followed me home from Sadie's that first night? Are you and Shawn partners … lovers … good friends … or what? Why were you watching me from your truck?"

Charley put her hands up, palms out, in a stop motion. "Give me a chance. I'll tell you everything." Settling herself in the chair beside the bed, she began. "First, they assigned me to check out a series of burglaries in your apartment complex.

"Apartments belonging to single people were systematically being robbed. The apartments weren't broken into, so we decided someone was either taking a chance picking locks or using a key. We thought it could be an inside job but didn't know the players.

"We spoke with Mrs. Keller, who acted as if it surprised her this was happening. She couldn't think of anyone who would have access to her keys. Moreover, she wanted us to believe she was upset about the whole thing. She didn't seem sincere, and she didn't seem to care about her tenants."

Janie shook her head. "I'm not surprised to hear that."

"I'm sure you're not. Every time we talked

to her, she tried to get information from us, instead of giving us anything."

"She is quite a gossip," said Janie. "I'm surprised she didn't tell you all kinds of things."

"Oh, she did," continued Charley, "things about various tenants. Who they were dating. Who had a new car. Who fought with their boyfriends or girlfriends. Anything, except information on the apartments that were burgled or those tenants. If she said anything it was somehow making the tenants look bad."

"So, what does this have to do with me?"

Several of the tenants, reported a black truck with tinted windows that sat outside their apartment. Most of them noticed it but assumed it was another tenant, possibly someone new."

Janie nodded, that's what she had thought. "As the robberies continued, the person in the truck became more and more brave. Flashing his lights, letting the tenant know he was watching them."

"That sounds familiar. But what about you? You have a black truck, and you were watching me. At least once."

"Let me come back to that. I told you Shawn is like a brother to me, and that's true."

Janie gave her a dismissive smirk and rolled her eyes. "Whatever. You sure seemed cozy at his mother's house."

"Don't jump to conclusions. Let me finish. My mother died when I was small. My dad had a tough time dealing with it. He became depressed and started drinking. Half the time, I didn't have anything to eat or wear. He didn't care if I went to school, if I combed my hair, or had a bath.

"Shawn's mom noticed and started taking care of me. I'd show up in time for dinner and she'd put another plate on the table without saying a word. Before I'd go home, she'd give me a bath and brush my hair. More often than not, she'd tuck me into a bed. She'd call my dad and tell him where I was. He didn't care.

Just one more thing he didn't have to deal with."

"I'm sorry you had such a terrible childhood. I guess we assume everyone else has it as well as we do."

"Especially when you're a kid. Most kids can't imagine a home without parents to take care of them." Charley took a deep breath and continued. "Anyway, Shawn was just a little older than I was. He understood my situation even though he was a kid himself. He started walking me to school and letting me tag around with him and his friends. If anyone gave me a hard time, or made fun of me, he would defend me. He really was like a big brother and I really needed one during that time."

"Later, in high school, I guess I had a crush on him and liked to think he was my boyfriend." Charley laughed, shaking her head. "He let me know in no uncertain terms that he was not my boyfriend. It hurt for a while, but then we went back to being friends. We became best friends.

We told each other everything, and we'd do anything for each other."

"Fast forward to Shawn meeting you—he was so taken with you. He fell for you faster than anyone he's ever dated."

Janie blushed. "I like him too."

"The day you met, Shawn called and told me about you. About you hitting him with a bagel and all. I asked questions like a sister would. He told me your address. He had looked it up to see if you have any priors and stuff."

Janie rolled her eyes. "Of course. Why not?"

Charley stood and started pacing the room as she continued. "Anyway, when he told me the address, I realized it was in the apartment complex that I was investigating. I told him what was going on and he immediately wanted to call and warn you."

"That would have been a good idea. Why didn't he?"

"I made him promise he wouldn't. I told him

I had been investigating and asked him to try to get some information for me since Mrs. Keller was no help."

"So, the two of you were using me?" Janie glared at Charley. "You put me in danger, so I could help you with your case?"

"No. Well, a little. It wasn't supposed to be that way."

The door flew open, and an enormous bouquet walked into the room. Peeking from behind it was Shawn.

"How are you feeling?"

"I'm doing well. The doc says I can go home soon. The flowers are beautiful." Janie gestured toward a small table in the corner of the room. "Pull that table over here so I can see them."

Shawn moved the table beside her bed but away from the IV stand and the tray table with the remains of her breakfast. They were lovely. Tall gladiolas, huge round sunflowers, balls of pink peonies, Russian sage, orange hostas, purple phlox, black-eyed susans. The flowers of summer gracefully gathered together in an unlikely mix.

"So many varieties. I would never have put them all together, but somehow they work." Janie threw her legs over the edge of the bed so she could get closer. She drew in a deep breath, inhaling the mix of fragrances. "Thank you, Shawn. They really are beautiful."

"I'm glad you like them, but more than that, I'm glad to see you doing so well this morning."

Janie grinned. "Charley has been telling me what really happened the last few weeks. She just informed me that the two of you decided to use me as bait to catch the bad guys."

"What? No! That's not true!" Shawn said defensively. He turned to Charley. "What are you telling her?"

"Tell me this, Charley, did you follow me home from the club the same day I met Shawn?"

"No, I didn't even know about you at that

point. That must have been Manuel."

"But why follow me from the club?"

"According to Manuel, Mrs. Keller had told him you were to be the next victim. He was supposed to keep an eye on you and find out your routine," said Charley. "He probably had followed you to the club as well as home. You just didn't realize it."

"Okay, but you were sitting in your truck in front of my apartment. We caught you out there."

"Yes, but that was a mistake. I sat outside several apartments many nights before I found out who would be next. The problem was, you found out I drove a black truck and decided it was the same truck that had been stalking you."

"Why didn't you just tell me the truth?"

"I did! I didn't lie to you. I just left out some details. I didn't want to take the chance it would get out that I was stalking the stalker!"

Janie jerked her head toward Shawn. "And

you! Why didn't you tell me? I trusted you! At least until you spent the night. You were acting so weird the next morning. Even weirder when we got to your parent's house. Then you showed up!" Janie's eyes shot toward Charley. "The two of you were all over each other. And you," she cut her eyes back to Shawn, "you were mean to me."

Shawn bowed his head sheepishly. "I'm not very good at acting. I really like you. I wanted to spend the day, just the two of us. But Charley called and told me she needed to meet with me about this case. She said not to tell you. We were supposed to act like friends, like ourselves. She wanted to come by and see if she could get more info from you. I really blew it."

"Yeah, you did," Charley chimed in. "I'm sorry, Janie. I know you left early because he was treating you so badly. I couldn't find a way to convince you to stay. We both blew it."

Janie shook her head in disbelief. "I wish

you would have told me the truth."

"Neither of us knew you well enough to risk the case." It was time for Charley to look sheepish. "Shawn wanted to tell you. I'm sorry."

The door opened again. This time, Heather walked in carrying a bag and a tall cup of coffee. Bruce followed behind with another cup of coffee, a small, wrapped gift, and a handful of balloons, one of which said, 'Happy Bar Mitzvah!'

"Good morning!" Heather bent down and gave Janie a hug. "I brought breakfast-" Then, glancing at her watch, "Or lunch! You look so much better. I thought we were going to lose you last night."

"Thanks a lot," said Jane. "Happy Bar Mitzvah?"

"Yeah, I know, but I thought it was pretty."

Heather handed Janie the bag of bagels and coffee. She took the balloons from Bruce and tied them to the foot of the bed.

"The way you looked last night, I was afraid you were dying. I mean, literally, dying!"

Bruce nodded; his eyes began to tear up. He sniffed, pulled out a tissue, and blew his nose. Without a word, he handed her the small package.

"You didn't have to buy me anything. I didn't die. See. Still alive and kickin'"

"Yeah, but you could have, and it would have been my fault," croaked Bruce.

"Your fault? What are you talking about? How would any of this be your fault? You set up my alarm system. You stood up to Manuel, and he's a big scary guy. But you didn't care, you just stepped up and zapped the crap out of him," said Janie. Bruce began to turn white.

"Yeah, then you used Judo to kick the gun out of Mrs. Keller's hand," said Heather. "Just think, your foot against her big powerful gun." Bruce began to swoon.

"I think I'm going to pass out," he said and crumbled to the floor.

Janie buzzed the nurse while the others fanned Bruce.

***

A few minutes later, everything was back to normal. Bruce was tucked into Janie's bed with an oxygen mask over his face. The nurse was taking his blood pressure. Janie had taken a seat in a chair the nurse brought in for her.

"Okay," Janie continued with her questions. "So how did all of you find me after Manuel grabbed me?"

"Well," said Heather, "it was like this. When we left last night, we noticed that black truck sitting in your parking lot again. I didn't think it was Charley and if it was, I wanted to catch her. I pointed it out to Bruce, who had an extra GPS tracking device in his glove compartment."

"I keep it there for emergencies," Bruce explained through the plastic oxygen mask.

"So, before we left, we attached it under the bumper of the truck. We figured we could follow the GPS and find out who was stalking you. Then the alarm went off, and the GPS started moving."

"How did you know the alarm went off?"

"Bruce programmed it to contact both the police and his watch," explained Heather. Bruce nodded.

"When the alarm went off, we were just a few blocks away, so we turned to come back, but then we noticed the dot on the GPS was moving, so we followed it. I kept trying to call you to see if you were okay and when you didn't answer, we were afraid they kidnapped you."

"How did the police find me?" Janie asked, amazed at the bravery of her friends.

"The alarm came into the station. I just happened to be there at the time," said Shawn. "When I heard the address, I knew it was you."

"He called me and told me about the alarm. I was going to meet him at your apartment. Then he called me back. Heather had called him and said she was chasing the black truck," Charley explained.

"Anyway, we told them to wait until we got there, but obviously, they didn't listen," said Shawn. "I'm thankful they didn't. If they hadn't gotten there when they did ..."

Janie saw tears forming in Shawn's eyes. He quickly brushed them away and cleared his voice.

"I think you know the rest," said Heather.

Janie's eyes began to tear as well. "I'm so thankful to all of you. This could have ended a lot differently. Because of you, I'm doing fine."

"Open Bruce's gift," said Heather.

"I almost forgot. Sorry, Bruce," said Janie.

Bruce nodded, his facemask fogging up as he exhaled a breath.

Janie carefully opened the small gift. It was a music box. "It's beautiful!" said Janie, admiring the intricate detail of the carvings on the mahogany base. She felt the key on the bottom and wound it up. As she opened the lid, she heard the delicate chimes playing the tune, *You've Got a Friend*.

Moved by the special sentiment of the gift, Janie wrapped her arms around Bruce. "You are definitely my friend." Looking around the room at the group who meant so much to her, she tried to tell them how she felt. "You all mean ..." her voice caught. Taking a breath, she swallowed the lump in her throat. "You all mean so much to me. I love you, every one of you."

Tears welled in the eyes of her friends. No one spoke. All were caught in the moment.

Once again, the door swung open.

"Are you ready to go home?" asked the doctor.

***

Together, they walked to the parking lot. Everyone silently engrossed in their own thoughts about the last several weeks, about last night, about relationships and about friendship.

"Do ya'll want to come to my place? I think I still have some *Jell-O* Fluff Salad?" asked Janie. The spell was broken. Everyone began talking at once, extolling the praises of Jell-O Fluff Salad.

ABOUT THE AUTHOR

Debbie Anderson currently lives in Ada, Oklahoma, with her two dogs, Sadie and Beethoven. She has three children, Josh, Janie, and Nathan, and four grandchildren, Austin, Sidney, Emerson, and Leila.

She has always enjoyed writing as a hobby. After surviving two bouts of cancer, one doctor suggested she write a book. This is her debut creation.

Debbie also enjoys sewing, quilting, painting, most crafts, and especially playing with her grandchildren and visiting family.

She hopes you enjoy this book and welcomes your comments at debbieanderson.writer1@gmail.com.

Made in the USA
Coppell, TX
12 January 2024